"I Never Understood Him
For A Moment,"

Giles said at last.

"As long as you understand him now—" Melanie began.

"But I don't. The only thing I have to hold on to is you. From the first moment, you've known what to say and do. It's strange—as though you and David were connected by an invisible thread."

Melanie tensed as he came so near her secret. But there was nothing but warmth in the smile he turned on her, and her heart gave the same disturbing lurch it had given before.

Dear Reader,

We all know that Valentine's Day is the most romantic holiday of the year. It's the day you show that special someone in your life—husband, fiancé...even your mom!—just how much you care by giving them special gifts of love.

And our special Valentine's gift to you is a book from a writer many of you have said is one of your favorites, Annette Broadrick. *Megan's Marriage* isn't just February's MAN OF THE MONTH, it's also the first book of Annette's brand-new DAUGHTERS OF TEXAS series. This passionate love story is just right for Valentine's Day.

February also marks the continuation of SONS AND LOVERS, a bold miniseries about three men who discover that love and family are the most important things in life. In *Reese: The Untamed* by Susan Connell, a dashing bachelor meets his match and begins to think that being married might be more pleasurable than he'd ever dreamed. The series continues in March with *Ridge: The Avenger* by Leanne Banks.

This month is completed with four more scintillating love stories: *Assignment: Marriage* by Jackie Merritt, *Daddy's Choice* by Doreen Owens Malek, *This Is My Child* by Lucy Gordon and *Husband Material* by Rita Rainville. Don't miss any of them!

So Happy Valentine's Day and Happy Reading!

Lucia Macro
Senior Editor

Please address questions and book requests to:
Silhouette Reader Service
U.S.: 3010 Walden Ave., P.O. Box 1325, Buffalo, NY 14269
Canadian: P.O. Box 609, Fort Erie, Ont. L2A 5X3

LUCY GORDON
THIS IS MY CHILD

SILHOUETTE *Desire*

Published by Silhouette Books

America's Publisher of Contemporary Romance

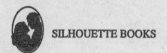 SILHOUETTE BOOKS

ISBN 0-373-05982-5

THIS IS MY CHILD

Copyright © 1996 by Lucy Gordon

LUCY GORDON

met her husband-to-be in Venice, fell in love the first evening and got engaged two days later. After twenty-three years they're still happily married and now live in England with their three dogs. For twelve years Lucy was a writer for an English women's magazine. She interviewed many of the world's most interesting men, including Warren Beatty, Richard Chamberlain, Sir Roger Moore, Sir Alec Guinness and Sir John Gielgud.

In 1985 she won the *Romantic Times* Reviewer's Choice Award for Outstanding Series Romance Author. She has also won a Golden Leaf Award from the New Jersey Chapter of RWA, was a finalist in the RWA Golden Medallion contest in 1988 and won the 1990 RITA Award in the Best Traditional Romance category for *Song of the Lorelei*.

One

Melanie sat in the hallway of Giles Haverill's luxurious house, and hated him.

She'd hated him for eight years, but never so much as at this moment, when she was about to meet him for the first time. She tried to fight down the feeling, knowing that the next few minutes would be the most crucial of her life. She must smile and say the things that would persuade this man to take her into his home. And he must never suspect that beneath her quiet exterior she was burning with hate.

The door to his study was pulled open and an unseen voice said curtly, "You can come in now, Miss Haynes."

She went inside and there was her enemy, reseating himself behind an oak desk strewn with papers. He was a large man, broad shouldered and dark haired, with a lean, handsome face set in a frown. Tension radiated from him. He looked her quickly up and down out of dark eyes that seemed to take in everything in one glance. Melanie trembled, afraid that he might look right into her heart and read her secret. But he merely grunted in a way that might have indicated approval of her neat clothes and pinned-back hair. He nodded her to a chair and put away some papers.

While he was occupied, she glanced around at the room. It was the office of a rich man, of plain if expensive tastes. The waste bin was made of steel, as was the lamp that hung over the desk. Where the walls weren't covered with steel shelving they were white, and bare except for two stark, modern paintings in vivid colors. The carpet was gray, and the most notable object in the room was a large sofa of soft black leather that exactly matched the seat behind the desk. The total effect was of a kind of austere beauty, but the room was chiefly functional, and it fitted her mental picture of Giles Haverill.

He looked up from his papers. "I was rather surprised to receive your call, Miss Haynes. It's true I was thinking of employing someone to care for my son, but I hadn't advertised yet."

"Somebody mentioned it at Ayleswood School," she said. "I'm working there at the moment."

"So you told me on the phone." He gave her a sharp look. "There are eighty pupils at that school. Would you have applied to look after any of the others?" he demanded abruptly.

"No—"

"Then why David?"

"I couldn't help noticing him—"

"Considering that he's been in trouble constantly for the last few months, that isn't surprising."

"I don't believe David is a naughty child," Melanie said quickly. "Just unhappy. Of course I know that his mother isn't here anymore—"

"His mother left me a year ago, for another man. She—didn't choose to take her son. I'm glad of that for my own sake, but it's had an unfortunate effect on David."

"I can imagine," Melanie said in a low voice.

"I wonder if you can picture just how bad it is." Giles Haverill's mouth twisted wryly. "Truancy, petty theft, lying—all the things that lead to delinquency later on if they're not curbed now."

"I should rather say, if they're not *cured* now."

Giles shook his head. "My son isn't ill, and I don't believe unhappiness excuses wrongdoing. I want to do everything I can to make him a happy child again, but that doesn't include turning a blind eye when he does things he shouldn't. No son of mine is going to grow up badly behaved because I didn't lift a finger to prevent it."

Melanie gripped her hands together out of sight, wondering how long she could conceal her dislike of this man with his harsh judgments. He spoke of making his child happy, but there was no love in his voice, just an iron determination to arrange things in the way he wanted.

"Did you know David was adopted?" Giles Haverill shot the question at her.

"The—school records didn't mention it," Melanie replied.

If he noticed her cautious choice of words he gave no sign. "My wife couldn't have children," he said. "Perhaps that's why she left him behind."

"Does he know he's adopted?"

"Yes. We told him as soon as he could understand. It seemed best for him to grow up knowing it naturally. But it adds to the problem now. He feels he's lost two mothers—if you can dignify the first one with the name of 'mother.' A woman who gives up her newborn child is beneath contempt. Don't you agree?"

"I—surely you should hear her side of it?" Melanie stammered.

"I don't think there can be any justification. However, let that pass. I must also tell you about Mrs. Braddock. She's a welfare worker who's taken far too close an interest in David since he's been misbehaving. She's been writing reports talking about how 'disturbed' he is, and how he needs to be 'closely observed.'" A sudden cloud of black anger transformed his face, and he said swiftly, "To dare say that my son— *my son...*"

Melanie stared, appalled at the rage that had distorted his handsome features. He looked cruel and ruthless, capable of anything. He saw her looking at him and recovered his composure. "She's started hinting about taking David into care, putting him with foster parents who could 'give him a normal home,' as she puts it."

"But he's used to you," Melanie protested. "Surely this woman can't think it will be good for him to lose you, as well as your wife?"

"That's what I said to her. But, as she pointed out, I haven't been around too much. I have a large business to run, and I've mostly left the care of David to Zena. When she left I thought I could manage, but it wasn't that easy." He saw her wry face and said sharply, "I'm not a 'New Man,' Miss Haynes. I don't pretend to be. I've tried to raise David as my father raised me, to have a sense of responsibility, and be able to take on the task of running Haverill & Son. It's a very big job and it needs a man trained virtually from the cradle."

"I see."

"I wonder if you do," he responded, quick to pick up the chilly note in her voice. "I made sure he had the best education money could buy because he's going to need it, and he justified my faith in him. Right from the start he was ahead of the class. In his nursery school he could read while the others were playing in the sand pit."

"I expect he knew there'd be hell to pay if he couldn't," Melanie couldn't resist saying.

"I've always let him know that my expectations of him were high. I think children respond to that. And he did respond—until recently. Now it's a story of truancy and idleness and frankly—"

"Frankly you feel he's letting you down," Melanie challenged him.

He looked at her hard for a moment. "Yes."

She'd meant to play it cool, but her temper was seething out of control. "Then I don't know why you don't let Mrs. Braddock have him. Unsatisfactory goods, to be returned."

"Because he's *mine*," he asserted bluntly.

"But he isn't, is he? Not by blood."

"Blood has nothing to do with it," he said, dismissing the whole of nature with an arrogant sweep of his hand. "He's mine because I say he's mine, because I've *made* him mine. And I don't let go of what's mine."

Their eyes met for a long moment. Then Giles Haverill recollected himself with a start, realizing that he'd come perilously close to defending and explaining himself. It was his rule never to do either of these things, but this young woman had lured him out from behind his

protective barriers in a few minutes. He had two con-
tradictory impulses: to get rid of her before she troubled him further, and to confide in her the hell of
confusion and misery in which he was living. He found
that he couldn't choose between them, which alarmed
him even more, because indecisiveness was foreign to
his nature.

"Coffee?" he asked, retreating to safety.

The abrupt change of subject caught her off guard.
"Thank you—er—yes—"

"I should have offered you some when you came in,
but I'm so distracted these days that I forget my manners." He went to a percolator by the wall and poured
her some. "Milk? Sugar?"

"Milk, no sugar, thank you."

"Tell me about yourself," he said when he'd served
her and sat down. "You said in your letter that you left
school at sixteen. No university?"

"It didn't attract me. I have two sisters and a brother,
who all went."

"But you were the odd one out? I wonder why." He
gave a sudden grin, which illuminated his face, giving
it a mocking look that was unexpectedly pleasing.
"Black sheep?"

"Yes," she said impulsively. "I was the naughty child
of the family. Everyone said so."

"So you and David have something in common.
Careful! Don't choke."

"I'm sorry," she gasped. "Went down—wrong way."

He waited until she was calm again. "What was the
matter? Did you mind my saying you and David had
something in common?"

She flinched from his penetrating eyes, afraid lest
they discern just how much in common she had with his

son. "Not at all," she said quickly. "I'm glad of it. I think David needs just the kind of understanding that I can give him. I know how naughtiness grows out of misery."

"Was your childhood as unhappy as that?"

"It's no fun being the black sheep."

"But that's all in the past. I'm sure your parents are proud of you now."

There was a long pause before Melanie said, "I'm not in touch with my family anymore—not for some years."

He waited to see if she would elaborate on this, but she didn't. He sat considering her for some moments, a frown darkening his face. Then he said abruptly, "I can't see you properly there. Come over here."

He rose and went to the big bay window. She followed him and stood in the light while he studied her. She too could see better now. He was in his mid-thirties, with a stern face that seemed made for authority. His mouth surprised her, being well made and mobile, a mouth that many women would have found attractive. It was relaxed now as he looked at her, and both from his mouth and his dark eyes, she gained an impression that this was an unhappy man. But she had no pity for him. He'd contributed too much to her own unhappiness for that.

"Take your hair down," he commanded.

"What?" She stared at him. "What difference does my hair make?"

"I don't make pointless requests. Please do as I ask."

She pulled the pins from her fair hair, letting it tumble in waves around her shoulders, and stared at him defiantly. He laid his hand on it, taking a strand between his fingers, savoring its silkiness. "It's lovely hair," he said quietly.

"I don't see what my physical attributes have to do with anything," she snapped.

"I think you do. That's why you pinned your hair back, to hide its beauty. That's why you don't wear makeup, because you want to look severe and professional. It doesn't work. You've got a lovely, delicate face, wonderful green eyes and a figure that must keep the men chasing after you." He said this in a cool, appraising voice that robbed the words of any tinge of flattery. "And you know as well as I do why I can't possibly employ you."

Her heart thundered. She recovered herself enough to say, "But I don't know."

"David needs stability. He needs a woman who'll stay with him through thick and thin. I had in mind somebody middle-aged, a widow or divorcée, perhaps with grown-up children, even grandchildren. You're a young, beautiful woman, which means you won't stay long."

"It doesn't mean that at all—"

"Oh, come! At your age the natural sequence of events is to fall in love and get married. I don't want you vanishing in a few months, just when he's learned to trust you."

"There's no question of that," Melanie said desperately.

"No question?" he echoed, with a satirical look that made her want to scream at him.

"No question whatever," she said, trying to speak calmly.

"You don't mean to tell me that there isn't a man in your life this minute?"

"There isn't."

"I don't believe you. The very gifts that nature gave you are an incitement. They don't affect me because I'm armored, but other men aren't. They must be around you like flies around a honey pot."

"Possibly," Melanie said, fighting to keep her temper. "But they don't get invited in. Any of them. Like you, Mr. Haverill, I'm armored."

"Oh, I see," he said grimly. "It's like that, is it?"

"I beg your pardon."

"When a woman renounces love it usually means she's suffering from a broken heart. Who is he? Is he going to come back and sweep you off?"

Melanie's eyes glinted with anger. "Mr. Haverill, this really isn't any of your business, but—"

"Everything is my business that I choose to make so."

"But the only time I imagined myself in love was nine years ago. And it'll be the last. You can count on it."

There was a long silence. She guessed he wasn't used to being answered back. Oh, God! she thought, don't let him refuse!

At last he said, "I'll have to take your word for that. I want someone who can make David feel safe and loved. Are you the woman who can do that?"

"Yes," she said, looking at him steadily. "I can do that as nobody else can."

He was startled by the intensity in her voice. Again he knew the inner prompting to get rid of her. She was dangerous. But he dismissed the notion as fanciful. "In that case," he said, "let's go and find him."

He led her out into the hall, toward the wide staircase.

Careful, she thought. Don't let Giles Haverill suspect that you've been in this house before, that you

know your way up these very stairs—the right turn at
the top toward the room at the end—it's the same room,
and the door's shut against you as it was before. . . .

A middle-aged woman in an apron was standing
outside the closed door, arguing with someone inside.
She looked up as they appeared. "I'm sorry, Mr. Haverill. David's locked himself in his room again."

He knocked hard on the door and called, "David,
come out here at once. You know I won't stand for this
behavior."

Melanie bit her lip. She wanted to cry out, "Don't
bully him. He's only a hurt, confused child." But she
said nothing.

"David."

Slowly the key turned in the lock and the door was
opened. The little boy who stood there was fair and
would have looked angelic but for the sullen defiance
written on his face.

"This is Miss Haynes," Giles said. "You've met her
before at school. She's to stay with us now, and look
after you."

There was no response. The child regarded her in a
silence that held no friendliness.

"David—" Giles began with an edge on his voice.

"Never mind," Melanie said. "There'll be plenty of
time."

He sighed. "All right. We'll discuss money in my office. When can you move in?"

"My job finishes in two days. I'll come immediately
after that."

"Fine. I'll have a room made ready for you."

She smiled at the little boy. "Goodbye, David. I'll be
back soon, and then we can get to know each other
properly."

Still saying nothing, the child backed into his room, keeping his eyes fixed on her. They were the eyes of a stranger, cold, withdrawn. The eyes of her son.

Late that night, in the bleak little flat where she lived alone, Melanie took out a photograph and studied it. It was battered from long use, frayed around the edges and stained with her tears. It showed a week-old baby sleeping in its mother's arms, and it was the only memento she had of the child she'd borne when she was sixteen.

She hadn't been married to the father. He'd vanished as soon as he learned of her pregnancy, but at that moment she hadn't cared. Her love for Peter, her baby, had been immediate, passionate and total. She would spend hours holding him, looking down into his face, knowing total fulfillment. As long as Peter needed her, nothing else mattered.

Even at that age he was an individual. While she smiled at him he would stare back, as grave as a little old man. Then his smile would break suddenly, like sun coming from behind clouds, always taking her by surprise and filling her with joy. For a while only the two of them existed in all the world.

Then her mother had said coolly, "It's time you decided to be sensible about this. Of course you can't keep the baby. It's a ridiculous idea."

"He's mine. I'm going to keep him," she cried.

"My dear girl, how? That layabout who fathered it has gone—"

"Peter isn't an 'it,'" she protested fiercely. "He's a person, and he's my son."

"Well, he wouldn't have been if you'd had the common sense to have an abortion. But I thought at least now you'd see how impossible the whole thing is."

"You could help me...." Melanie pleaded.

But her mother had raised four children and considered she'd 'done her bit.' Besides, she had a job now, one that she liked. She made it plain that her baby-minding days were in the past.

"Then I'll look after him by myself. I'll get a flat—"

"Oh, yes, a flat—in some ghastly high-rise block with an elevator that never works and the stairs littered with syringes, living off welfare payments that aren't enough. You say you love him. Is that the life you want for him?"

Dumbly Melanie shook her head while tears began to roll down her cheeks, and she held onto her child more tightly than ever. She hadn't yielded at once, but the euphoria of the first few days was insidiously being replaced by postpartum depression.

In the blackness that seemed to swirl around her after that, only one thing remained constant, and that was her love for Peter. She breast-fed him, pouring out her adoration as she poured out her milk, clinging to the hope that something would happen to let her keep her baby.

But it didn't. Instead there was the constant verbal battering from her family, always on the same theme, "If you loved him you'd give him up—a child needs two parents—a better life—if you loved him you'd give him up."

At last, distraught, deep in depression, barely knowing what she was doing, she signed the papers and said goodbye to her child. For six months the conviction of doing the right thing supported her. And then, with brutal timing, the clouds lifted from her brain on the day after the adoption was finalized by the court, and with dreadful clarity she saw what she'd done.

The separation from her baby was an agony that wouldn't heal. Her desperate pleas to be told where he was were met with bland official statements about confidentiality. All the legal processes had been completed. It was too late for her to change her mind.

Her last hope was a friend who worked for the council and who broke all the rules to give her the names, Mr. and Mrs. Haverill, and an address. Frantically she raced to their house to plead with them, only to find that Giles Haverill had already left the country to start a new firm in Australia, as part of the business empire he ran for his father. His wife, Zena, was in the middle of final packing. If Melanie had hoped to find an understanding maternal heart, she was bitterly disappointed. Zena Haverill was a strong-featured young woman with a cold voice, who had no intention of giving up what she considered hers.

"There are other babies," Melanie pleaded.

"Other babies? My dear girl, do you know how hard it is to get a baby these days? Now I've got David, there's no way I'm going to give him back."

"His name's Peter."

"Giles, my husband, prefers David, after his own father. He's a very rich man, you know. David will have the best of everything, and I daresay he'll be better off than with an unmarried and—if you'll pardon my saying so—rather unstable young woman. Look, I'll lay it on the line because I'm tired of arguing. I can't have children myself, and David is exactly what Giles wants."

"Giles—Giles," Melanie raged. "You don't say that *you* want him."

"There's no need to discuss this," Zena Haverill said coolly, and something in her voice told Melanie the terrible truth.

"You don't want him, do you?" she accused. "Your husband wants an heir, that's all it is. *You don't love him.*"

"I see nothing to be gained by hysteria. David will have every advantage."

"But he won't have a mother who loves him," Melanie screamed. "Oh, God! *Oh, God!*"

Zena regarded her dispassionately. "The welfare worker told me you gave up David because you wanted to play in a rock band. I can only say that if this performance is anything to go by you should have been an actress. However, it doesn't move me, you know."

"Rock band?" Melanie echoed, dazed. "I don't know what you mean. I may have mentioned to her that I once thought of something like that, but I didn't give Peter up because of it. I don't care about a career now. I just want my baby."

"*My* baby," Zena said calmly. "Mine and my husband's. Now I think you'd better go."

She'd pleaded for one last sight of Peter, a chance to say goodbye, but Zena had been like flint.

"He hasn't seen you for months. You'd only disturb him. Besides," she added belatedly, "he isn't here."

"He is, I can hear him."

She ran out of the room, up the stairs toward the sound of a baby's crying. In her distraught state it seemed that Peter was calling to her. But she never got to him. A nurse came out of a room at the end of the corridor, closed it firmly behind her and stood with her back to it.

"*Peter,*" Melanie screamed. "*Peter.*"

Then Zena caught up with her, and together she and the nurse wrestled her downstairs into the hall.

"I suggest you leave now before I call the police and charge you with attempted kidnapping," Zena said breathlessly.

She'd stumbled out of the house, tears streaming down her cheeks. As the front door was slammed shut, she turned and screamed, "He's my baby. I'll get him back, whatever I have to do."

But the next day Zena had gone to Australia, taking Peter with her.

Melanie had tried to put the past behind her and plan for a career. She'd been a talented pianist and for a while she *had* played keyboard with a rock band that had some modest success. Men pursued her, attracted as much by her haunting air of melancholy as by her gentle beauty. But she had nothing to give them. The trauma she'd been through had frozen her, until now she was sure she would never fall in love. Only one kind of feeling still lived in her, and it was one she couldn't acknowledge. Each year she celebrated Peter's birthday with a breaking heart, and each night she prayed for a miracle.

At last the rock band broke up. Melanie was growing weary of the futility of the life and she left music completely to take business courses. She joined a temping agency and took a succession of jobs until at last she was hired for a month by Ayleswood School, a select, fee-paying establishment, whose secretary was off sick. And there she found her miracle, in the school records.

His name was David Haverill, son of Giles and Zena Haverill, and his address was the very same house where she'd confronted Zena. There could be no doubt. The family had returned from Australia, and now her child was here, within a few yards of her.

When her first transports of joy had calmed, she began to search for him slowly, careful not to attract attention. There were three boys who were possible. None of them had her features, or Oliver's, but they were fair haired, like herself. She'd cherished dreams of an instant thunderbolt of recognition, but it didn't happen that way.

It happened through stealing.

he'd come into the anteroom of the headmistress's o ice one afternoon to find one of the "possibles" there. He was sitting on the edge of a seat, his face set in a mask that might have concealed defiance or indifference or just plain misery. "Hello," Melanie said cautiously. "I've got some files for Mrs. Grady. Do you know if she's in there?"

He stared at her for a long moment before nodding. "She told me to wait here," he said at last.

"I'm Melanie. What's your name?'

"David."

Her heart began to hammer. "David Haverill?" she asked breathlessly.

He nodded again. He seemed strangely listless for a boy of eight.

"Are you here because you're in trouble?" she asked gently.

For the first time, he raised his head and looked at her directly. His nod was almost imperceptible and his eyes were wary.

"Well, I don't suppose it's so very bad," she said in a rallying voice.

Before he could speak, the headmistress had opened her door and said, "You can come in now, David."

Melanie had been forced to leave the files she'd brought and depart, trying to look indifferent to conceal her inner turbulence. After all these years she'd found her son.

She had to wait until next morning to find out more. When she casually mentioned the incident and asked what had brought David to the office, Mrs. Grady, the headmistress, said, "Stealing, and not for the first time. I suppose we shouldn't blame the child too much. He never acted like this before his mother went away."

"Went away?" Melanie asked.

"Ran off and left the poor little mite, about a year ago."

Something was constricting Melanie's breathing. "And—his father?"

Mrs. Gray's voice became tart with disapproval. "I had to get his father out of a board meeting yesterday to tell him what had happened. He wasn't pleased. Oh, I think he's fond of the boy in a business-must-come-first sort of way, and he used to be proud of him. But frankly he's not coping very well, either, and if he doesn't start managing better he may lose David entirely."

"But why?" Melanie asked, startled. "Lots of fathers bring up children alone these days."

"It's not that. David's run away twice, trying to find his mother. Once he was gone for two days. We had to call the police out to search for him. So of course the social services became involved, and then they discovered about the stealing, as well. To them he looks like a disturbed child. He actually has a social worker assigned to him, and I know she doesn't think Giles Haverill is doing a marvelous job of giving David the reassurance he needs."

That night Melanie dreamed Peter was calling to her again. The baby she'd heard crying eight years ago and the little boy who'd run away to find his mother merged into one child, pleading for her to go to his rescue. She awoke with her mind already made up. Fate had offered her the chance she'd prayed for, to be reunited with her son, even if it meant being his nanny, not his mother.

She went about her plans with cool determination. There could be no failure. While learning secretarial skills she'd sometimes worked as a baby-sitter. Now she contacted the parents for references, and when she had them she telephoned Giles Haverill.

Confronting the man himself was the hardest part. Melanie's dislike of Zena was a rational thing, based on their meeting. But over the years Giles had loomed in her mind as a monster, the unseen puppet master whose demand for an heir had made his wife grasp at a child she didn't love.

Now she was over that hurdle. Giles Haverill was no longer a monster, but a stern, unlikable man. He'd sized her up like goods to be assessed before buying, and she'd tolerated it because she had her eyes on her goal. There would be other things to put up with, but she would endure them all. This was her chance, and she was going to take it, Giles Haverill or no Giles Haverill.

Two

The room that Melanie had been allocated was right next to David's. It was spacious and pleasant, and Brenda, the middle-aged housekeeper, had made it spotless.

"Thank goodness you're here, Miss," she said as she showed Melanie the room. "I've had all I can take of that child. He's a right little devil. He's rude and awkward, shuts himself in his room for hours at a time, and when he does come out, half the time he won't talk."

"Perhaps he's got nothing to say," Melanie observed, disliking Brenda.

"Humph! Last week all my dusters went missing. Every single one. He'd hidden them under his bed, just for the fun of watching me chasing around."

Melanie laughed. "That doesn't sound so very wicked, just normal childish mischief."

"And there's the staring."

"What do you mean?"

"He stares at you as though he could see right through you. Just stares on and on. It's unnerving."

"Does he have any friends?"

"Not anymore. He made some at school, I think, but since he became a thief—"

"Don't call him a thief," Melanie said quickly.

"What else do you call a kid who steals? You do know he steals, don't you?"

"I don't think it's a good idea to hang labels around a child's neck," Melanie said firmly.

Brenda shrugged. "Please yourself. But be sure to hide your things away."

A shadow darkened the door. Melanie looked up to see Giles. "When you've finished settling in, Miss Haynes, perhaps you'd come down to my office."

He departed without waiting for an answer. Melanie went down a few moments later and found him regarding her dispassionately. "Perhaps I should make it plain at the outset that your duties will not include listening to Brenda slandering my son," he snapped.

"I think my duties include anything that will help David," she said calmly. "And first of all that means learning all I can about his problems."

"I can tell you everything you need to know."

"Can you? There's probably a lot about him *you* don't know. Why not let me approach him my own way?"

He considered her thoughtfully. "Very well," he said at last in a dismissive voice. "But I don't want to overhear any more conversations like that."

She was turning away, confirmed in her poor opinion of him, when he stopped her. "Miss Haynes..."

There was an uncertain note in his voice that took her by surprise.

"Yes?"

"Those dusters—it *was* just childish mischief, wasn't it? The sort of thing any boy of his age might do." He was almost pleading.

"Exactly the sort of thing I did when I was a child. I told you I was the black sheep. Can you tell me where to find David?"

"In the garden."

The garden was huge and could have been an enchanted place for a crowd of children, but it dwarfed one solitary little boy. David was sitting on a log, absently tossing sticks. Melanie was sure he detected her approach, but he refused to raise his head as she crossed the grass toward him.

"Hello," she said cheerfully.

He continued tossing twigs, ignoring her presence.

"Do you remember me?" she persisted.

At last he raised his head to look at her silently, and she understood what Brenda had meant about his staring. "My name's Melanie," she said. "And I know you're David. It's nice to meet you properly at last." A sudden impulse made her put out her hand, and she said, "How do you do?" as she would have done with an adult.

After watching her carefully for a moment, he took her hand. "How do you do?" he said politely.

"Has your father told you very much about me?" she asked, feeling her way by inches.

"Yes. He says it'll be like having Mommy back, but *it won't.*"

On the last words his voice rose to a sudden shout that made her flinch. She stared at him, appalled. For a moment the mask had cracked, giving her a glimpse of the rage and misery that boiled beneath. "Of course it won't," she said quickly. "Daddy didn't mean that I could take Mommy's place." It hurt to speak of Zena as his mother but she had no time for her own feelings now. "He just meant that I'd be here if you ever needed me."

"I don't need you," he said coldly. "I don't need anyone. I don't need Mommy or Daddy, or you or *anyone.*" Again there was that unnerving shout, coming out of nowhere.

"Well, perhaps you don't," she said, as if giving the matter serious consideration. "But maybe Daddy needs *you.* Have you thought of that?"

He shook his head. "Daddy doesn't need me."

"Why do you say that?"

"Because I'm bad."

The bald statement brought tears to her eyes. She fought them back. "Don't call yourself bad. It isn't true."

"Yes, it is. Everyone says so."

Mercifully memory came to her rescue. "I was bad, too," she said, trying to sound cheerful. "One of my teachers told my parents I was on my way to becoming a juvenile delinquent."

"What's a ju...ju...?"

"Juvenile delinquent? Someone who causes chaos. I did things that made that duster trick look like nothing."

"Brenda was really mad," he said with satisfaction.

"Yes, it's no fun if they don't get mad," she agreed.

A glimmer of appreciation appeared in his eyes. "What sort of things did you used to do?"

"There was a boy in my class who used to bully anyone smaller than himself," she recalled. "He made people's lives a misery. I sat behind him one day and painted his hair with glue." She chuckled. "It wouldn't wash out. He had to cut the hair off. Of course his parents complained to mine, and I was in trouble. But it was worth it. There's a lot of fun to be had with sticky stuff."

He didn't answer this, but she was pleased to notice that he was looking more cheerful. When she asked him to show her around the garden he got up at once. He was knowledgeable for a boy of his age, and talked to her about his surroundings in a way that made her start to feel hopeful.

But her mood was short-lived. After lunch she had to return to her old flat to collect a bag she'd overlooked. Brenda agreed to look after David and take him shopping with her. David too seemed happy to go shopping, which puzzled Melanie slightly, as it seemed odd for this activity to appeal to a small boy.

But she returned to find a message that she was to see Giles immediately. In his study he turned exasperated eyes on her. "You've only been here a day," he snapped, "and already you've shown David new ways to make life hideous for the rest of us."

"I beg your pardon?" she said blankly.

"It was you who told him how much 'fun' could be had with 'sticky stuff,' wasn't it?"

"Oh, heavens! What's he done?"

"Ask Brenda."

"He didn't glue her hair, did he?" Melanie asked, horrified.

"Not her hair. Her purse. She went to pay the paper bill and found her purse stuck solid."

Melanie gasped and caught her lip between her teeth. "That was wrong of him, of course," she said in a shaking voice. "Very naughty."

"Then you can be the one to tell him so."

"I'm sure you've already told him."

"But he needs to hear it from you, since you seem to be his partner in crime," Giles said grimly.

"David!" She'd spied him lurking in the hall, and called to him. He came nearer, watching her closely, as though waiting for the storm. "Come here, you wretch," she said cheerfully. "Now see what you've done to me."

"But you said—"

"I did it to a boy in school who'd been bullying people. He was a fair target. Brenda isn't. It wasn't kind of you to make her life hard. Come on, let's go and tell her you're sorry."

"But I'm not sorry," he said innocently.

"Then fake it," she told him, leading him away with a hand on his shoulder.

Brenda greeted them frostily but received David's mumbled apology in astonishment. "And I'm sorry, too," Melanie said before the housekeeper could recover. "I put the idea into his head, but I didn't mean to. I'll be more careful in the future."

They came out of the kitchen to find Giles in the hall. "I only came home to get my things," he explained. "I have to fly to New York. The plane leaves in a couple of hours." He was shrugging on his coat as he spoke, and Melanie saw his bags standing by the front door. "It's lucky you're here or I'd have had a problem about leaving."

"Will you be away for long?" she asked.

"I've no idea, but it'll give you a chance to get to know David. You're in sole charge." He turned to David. "I've got to go now, son. You'll behave yourself, won't you? Don't give Miss Haynes any trouble. I shall expect good reports of you when I return."

To hell with good reports, Melanie thought crossly. Tell him you'll miss him.

David hadn't spoken. He stood next to Melanie in silence, but as Giles headed for the door he suddenly dashed forward and clasped his father, hiding his face against him. Melanie tensed, ready to hate Giles if he pushed his son away, but he didn't. To her surprise he dropped onto one knee and put an arm around David. "Hey, come on now," he said in a rallying voice. "It's not for long." David didn't answer in words but his arms went around his father's neck. "It's all right, son," Giles said in a softer voice than Melanie had heard him use before. "I'm coming back."

Then he enfolded David in a fierce hug, burying his face in the child's soft fair hair. When he emerged, his voice was a little husky, but that might have been the effect of being half strangled. "Goodbye," he said quickly, and went away, leaving Melanie wondering just what sort of a man he really was.

Giles was away for a week, and it was a happier week than Melanie had known for a long time. She was in David's company every day. It was she who took him to school, collected him, had tea with him, put him to bed. It was what she'd dreamed of for years, and at first it was enough.

She was free to slip into his room at night and watch him sleeping, hugging her joy to herself like a miser brooding over rediscovered gold. She'd often wondered how the reunion would be. Would her heart still recognize him as her son?

But all was well. On her side the bond held, true and strong, and along it streamed love as fierce and protective as the love he'd once drunk in with her milk. She instinctively knew that this was the child she'd held in her arms so long ago. When he wasn't looking her way, she would watch him in secret, inwardly whispering words of wonder, "My son. My son."

But as the days slipped past she knew that she hadn't made the breakthrough she wanted. David spoke to her politely enough, but he didn't give her the eager confidence she longed for, and she could sense that he was still wary of her. She was inching her way along, always alert to seize the moment that might bring them closer, but such moments were painfully slow in coming.

One morning she heard Brenda grumbling inside David's room. "... think I've got nothing better to do than change sheets every day."

"Is anything the matter?" Melanie asked, entering.

"He's done it *again*," Brenda declared bitterly. "Look at that!" She held up a sheet with a large damp place. "It's time he pulled himself together instead of acting like a baby."

David's face was scarlet and he was fighting back the tears. Melanie put a hand on his shoulder. "Go down to the garden," she suggested gently. "And don't worry. It's not important."

She shut the door behind him and faced Brenda. "From now on if David is unlucky enough to wet his bed, you tell me and no one else. I won't have him made to feel bad about it."

Brenda was up in arms, her heavy face mottled with anger. "He's not the only one who feels bad. It's me who has to do the extra washing."

"Aided by a state-of-the-art washing machine," Melanie said, her temper rising. "If putting a few sheets in it is too much for you, I'll do it. But the important thing is that you are to say nothing to David. Do you understand?"

Brenda seemed about to argue but then fell silent, alarmed by a fierce gleam in Melanie's eyes. She wasn't to know that she was dealing with a tigress defending her cub. She only knew that something in the other woman's look quelled her. She sniffed and hurried out of the room.

Melanie joined David in the garden and said, "Don't worry about Brenda. She won't bother you anymore."

"I'm not a baby," David said quickly.

"Of course you're not."

"But Daddy says I am," he told her in a wobbly voice.

She put a hand on his shoulder. "You leave Daddy to me."

He looked at her in awe. Then a smile of gratitude and trust came over his face.

"Come on," she said. "What are we going to do today?"

He slipped a hand in hers. "I've got a new computer game," he said eagerly.

"Come on, then. Teach me."

They spent the day cheerfully zapping each other on the screen. Like many children of his generation, David was at ease with computers and instructed Melanie with careful courtesy. One moment he was like a little old-fashioned gentleman, the next he was doubled up with excitement and laughter. But then he would grow suddenly quiet, as though all the computer games in the world couldn't ease the crushing burden on his heart.

Late that evening the telephone rang. Melanie lifted the receiver in her bedroom and found herself talking to Giles.

"Is everything all right?" he said. "Is David behaving himself?"

"Perfectly. He'll be thrilled that you called him. Just a moment." She hurried out of her room to knock on David's door. "He's just coming," she said when she returned to the phone."

"Actually I didn't—if you hadn't run off so fast I could have told you that all I meant—" He sighed.

I know you weren't going to talk to David, Melanie thought crossly. That's why I called him before you could stop me.

David bounced in. "Is it really Daddy?"

"That's right," Melanie said brightly. She added, loud enough for Giles to hear, "He called especially to talk to you."

"Hello, Daddy—*Daddy*—"

Listening to the child's end of the conversation, Melanie formed the impression that Giles was laboring to keep going. He seemed to be questioning David about his behavior when he ought to have been saying how much he missed him. But David's delight was touching.

At last he said, "Yes, Daddy, I'll be good. Goodbye."

"Back to bed now," Melanie commanded with a laugh.

It took time to settle him down again. In his excitement at receiving his father's call, he repeated everything that had been said a dozen times. But at last he snuggled down between the sheets and dropped off. Melanie crept out of the room but couldn't resist returning an hour later. The moon, sliding between a crack in the curtains, touched David's face, revealing a smile of blissful content that she had never seen before.

Melanie stood looking at that innocent smile for a long time, hating Giles Haverill with all her heart.

During weekdays, when David was at school, Melanie took the chance to explore the house. It had been built about sixty years earlier by the first Haverill to make money, and had a look of forbidding prosperity. The design was spacious but undistinguished, and the best part of the place was the huge garden. Someone had designed that garden with love, arranging trees and shrubs so that there were constant surprises and changes of view.

Downstairs the big piano tempted her. It was locked, but after a search she found the key on a hook behind the door of Giles's office. Playing again was like rediscovering a lost friend. She sat there for so long that she was nearly late fetching David from school, and had to hurry. When she told him what had delayed her, he stared. "Daddy keeps the piano locked," he said. "He stopped my lessons."

"Why did he do that?" she asked gently.

He didn't reply. His face was set in the rigid lines of misery she'd seen on the day she first saw him at school. "It was my own fault," he said at last.

After tea she asked him to play for her. As soon as he started, she realized that he had a talent and confidence that were like her own at the same age. Listening to her child expressing himself through the gift that had always been hers, Melanie breathed a prayer of thanks. "You ought to be in the school concert," she said when he'd finished.

"I was going to, but Daddy said no. He says if I can't get my schoolwork right . . . it's next week." he finished miserably. "And everyone's in it except me."

Melanie drew a long breath and counted to ten to stop herself expressing her opinion of Giles in terms unsuitable for a child's ears. "Let me hear it again," she begged. "You do it so well."

He gave her a smile, full of delight and a kind of wonder at receiving praise, and started again from the beginning. While she listened, Melanie's mind was working furiously.

The following afternoon she sought out Mrs. Harris, the school music teacher, and found in her an ally. "Giles Haverill . . ." she said with concentrated loathing, then checked herself. "I'm sorry, I know he's your employer—"

"Don't stop on my account," Melanie said. "I don't like him, either. But he left me in charge of David and I'd like him to be in the concert. With any luck Mr. Haverill won't even be back until it's over."

David's joy, when she told him, was so great that she thought he would fling his arms about her. But the moment passed, and he retreated behind the barrier of caution with which he protected himself.

She began to practice the piece with him. She never had to tell him anything twice. These were their happiest times together. It was an effort not to reach out and stroke the shiny fair head bent earnestly over the piano. It was even harder not to gather him up in a hug.

But the painful years had taught her patience. She must wait for that hug.

"Try it again," she said one evening. "I love listening to you."

He went through the piece easily, smiling at her as he mastered a tricky place, and she smiled back. They were sitting like that when Giles walked in.

"What's this?" he asked quietly.

They both looked up quickly, and Melanie felt David flinch and move toward her. His lips moved in the word "Daddy!" but his voice was nervous.

Giles's face was very pale, and his lips were set in a hard line. It seemed to Melanie that his face showed only anger. She didn't know that he'd heard his son's whispered word, seen him recoil, and felt as though something had struck him in the chest.

"Aren't you going to say hello to me, son?" he asked.

David slipped obediently from the piano stool and went across to Giles, who went down on one knee to look him full in the face. David put his arms about his father, but it seemed to Melanie that he did so reluctantly. Giles felt it, too, and hardened himself against the hurt. When he arose his face was grim. "Who unlocked the piano?" he asked.

"I did," Melanie said. "And I need to talk to you. I'll come to your study when I've put David to bed."

As they walked out of the room, he heard her saying, "Don't worry, David. Everything will be all right, I promise."

There was a protective note in her voice, Giles noted. She was protecting David against *him*.

In his study he poured himself a stiff brandy and waited for her, not at all relishing the way she'd taken the initiative in this meeting. It occurred to him that he disliked this woman. When she appeared, her face bore none of the unease he was used to seeing in his subordinates when they presented themselves for criticism. "What the devil do you think you're doing?" he demanded. "How dared you encourage him to defy me!"

"And how dared you break that child's heart by denying him one of the few comforts he has!" she flung back. "How could you be so cruel, so callous?"

"I have good reasons for what I do—"

"There are no good reasons for hurting an eight-year-old child," she said firmly.

He paused to take a long breath, but before he could hurl his anger and bitterness at her he was swamped by weariness. He sat down abruptly and closed his eyes, and the words that came out of his mouth, much against his will, were, "I haven't slept for forty-eight hours." He pulled himself forcibly together. "I don't know what David's told you—"

"The truth. He's a very honest boy. He says you stopped his lessons because he got behind at school. Naturally he blames himself."

"Why naturally?"

"Because he blames himself for everything that happens. Didn't you know that?"

He shook his head, dumbly. He had a great longing to close his eyes.

"He told me how you'd pulled him out of the concert, too," Melanie said. "I was astonished. I'd have thought you would seize the chance to boost David's confidence, and give him an hour of happiness that will help him cope with the past dreadful year."

"I see. So what did you do, Miss Haynes? For I feel very sure that you did something."

"I put him back in the concert. He's so happy about it that for the last two nights he hasn't even wet his bed. And *that's* made him even happier. But of course you can always go up and tell him that it's all off."

He eyed her shrewdly. "You're a very clever woman."

"Are you going to do that—and break his heart?"

"Of all the disgracefully loaded questions—!" he exploded. "Look, if I agree to this concert, there must be no more encouraging him to defy me. We have to lay down some ground rules, and you must abide by them. I'm glad you and David seem to get along well, but he's *my* son, not yours. Is that understood?"

"Perfectly," she said in a colorless voice.

"Very well. Now we've got that clear, he can do the concert."

"And you'll be there?"

"What?"

"It's a pity that we can't tell him you rushed home on purpose to see him, but it's a bit late for that now. Never mind, we'll have to make the best of it."

"Good of you," he said shortly. But irony was lost on her, he realized. "It's out of the question. I'm behind on my appointments because I've been away. I can't take an evening off. Is David's life really going to be blighted if I don't come to listen to him playing the piano in a drafty school hall?"

"His life will be blighted if you don't show him that he's vitally important to you."

"I do that every day—"

"Not in ways that mean anything to him. He's *eight*. He doesn't care that you're out there building an industrial empire, but he does care that you treat his big moment as though it mattered. Weren't you ever in a school performance?"

"For pity's sake! I don't recall my parents turning out to my school functions. It hasn't damaged me."

She looked at him levelly. "Well, you know best about that, of course."

He took a deep breath. "What's the exact date? I'm too jet-lagged to work it out."

She told him, crossing her fingers for the miracle. But it didn't come. "I'm sorry," he said. "There's a banquet on that night—it's what I came back for—I'm making a speech—there are going to be government ministers there—for heaven's sake, surely you can understand?" His voice rose in irritation.

"Of course," she said crisply. "I understand perfectly. So will David. Good night, Mr. Haverill."

When she'd gone, he sat staring into space, a prey to turbulent emotions. Pictures danced before him—David sitting at the piano, his head close to that woman, exchanging smiles with her. His flinching at the sight of his father. It had been a mistake to let her into the house. He'd known that on the day they met. She'd stood there in the bay of the window, with the light falling on her lovely face and deep, mysterious eyes, and he'd been filled with alarm. He didn't know why he should be afraid of this young woman, who seemed to have an immediate empathy with David. After all, that was what he'd hoped for when he hired her. But he had the feeling of having released a genie that had got far beyond his control. And tonight, when he'd seen David turn to her, seeking refuge from his own father, he'd known that by some mysterious process she was stealing his son.

He passed a hand over his eyes, wishing his head didn't ache so.

Three

On the afternoon of David's concert, Giles said to Melanie, "I thought a lot about what you said—about David needing his parents there to cheer him on."

"Yes?" she urged eagerly.

"So I called Zena this morning, to see if she would go. But all I got was the answering machine saying they were away for a few days."

She sighed. "Well, it looks as though David will have to make do with me."

"I just wanted you to know that I tried," he said, and even to his own ears his voice sounded hollow.

To the last minute, she clung to the hope that Giles would change his mind, but when she saw him descend the stairs in white tie and tails she knew he hadn't dressed up for a school concert.

David, too, was ready to leave. Giles placed a hand on

his son's shoulder. "Good luck," he said. "Make me proud of you."

"Yes, Daddy." David's voice was expressionless and his face had become a mask again. Melanie threw an angry look at Giles, but he was already walking away and didn't see it. She wanted to shout after him, "How can you be proud of him if you're not there?"

Then she wondered at her own thoughts. She would have David's big moment all to herself, free from Giles Haverill's intrusion. As his mother, what more could she ask?

But it wasn't enough. She wasn't the one David wanted. Giles might be neglectful, overbearing and insensitive, but his little son adored him and lived for his praise. And she, who loved David more than anything in life, wanted only his happiness.

In the school hall she made sure of getting a seat where David could see her, and led the applause when he appeared. She held her breath as he played the opening notes. Then gradually she relaxed as she realized everything was going to be fine. He played confidently, without stumbling once, and when he reached the end the applause was more than just polite.

"Well done," she said when they met afterward. "That was the best ever."

"Would Daddy be proud of me?" he asked wistfully.

"Of course he will. I'm going to tell him how splendid you were."

At home she gave him some milk and sandwiches, and put him to bed. He snuggled down, promising to go to sleep, but when she came up later she heard noises from inside his room. She listened for a moment before pushing the door open a crack. David's little television was on. "You shouldn't be watching that now," she said.

"But I'm watching Daddy," he pleaded. "Look."

As Melanie glanced at the screen the announcer was saying, "... *made a speech to captains of industry tonight, in which he declared...*" There was Giles talking from the top table to a room full of men, all identically dressed in white tie and tails. David's eyes never left the screen. "That's Daddy!" he said excitedly.

Sure enough, there was Giles, at ease, speaking without notes. Seeing him like this, Melanie realized how handsome he was. When he made a neat joke, his white teeth gleamed against the brown of his skin. He was in the prime of life, assured, at ease, a master in his own sphere. But none of that was of any use to the little boy who had to watch him through a television screen.

When the program was over she persuaded him to lie down. "Tomorrow we'll talk about what we're going to do during your school holidays. Will your father be taking you away on vacation?"

He shrugged. "Don't know."

"What about your mother?" Melanie asked cautiously.

He looked back at her from unblinking eyes. "My mother's dead," he said simply.

Melanie expelled her breath slowly, realizing that she'd wandered into a mine field. Who had told the child that Zena was dead, and why hadn't Giles warned her? "Well..." she began to say.

"My mother's dead," David repeated. "If she wasn't dead I'd be living with her."

"I see. Yes, of course. Do you—have a photograph of her anywhere?"

"No," David said. "She's dead. She's *dead.*"

Again there was that unnerving stare. Melanie had an impression that inside himself the little boy was clinging onto a sheer cliff face with his fingertips. "Good night," she said softly, and left him.

She went to her own room and did some thinking. And when her thinking was completed she settled down to wait for Giles Haverill's return, because no matter how late he was, she needed to talk to him urgently.

To pass the time, she switched on the television and found herself watching a late news program. It ran a brief clip of Giles's speech, followed by some general information about his earlier career.

"Haverill & Son has always been a family firm," declared the presenter, "but under Giles Haverill it became one of the major operators in the sphere of—"

Melanie hardly heard. She was studying Giles as he'd been a few years ago, his face already set in stern lines, his eyes fixed ahead as though nothing mattered but his goal. Sometimes he was accompanied by a woman Melanie recognized as Zena, but mostly he was shown heading meetings and traveling by airplane, concentrating on the screen of a portable computer.

"...a ruthless operator, as more than one of his rivals could testify—pride in the firm he inherited, and his determination to double it in size and influence—"

"And to raise his son to do the same," Melanie murmured. "Poor little mite."

She looked angrily at the face on the screen, the face of a conqueror, an acquisitor, a man so proud of his heritage that he'd trained a child from birth to fit into it.

"And I handed you over to him," she whispered angrily. "God forgive me!"

As the hours ticked away she began to doze off. To keep herself awake, she went out into the hall and settled on the stairs. She was awakened about two in the morning by the sound of the front door opening and closing. "Miss Haynes?" Giles called, peering into the gloom of the hall. "What are you doing on the stairs?"

Melanie yawned and got stiffly to her feet. "I wanted to be sure not to miss you, Mr. Haverill. There are things we have to discuss."

"Can't it wait until tomorrow?"

"No, it can't. I need to get some things straightened out before I see David again."

"Look," he said tiredly, "I'll pay for it, whatever he's done."

"He hasn't done anything. Can we talk somewhere more private than the hall?"

"All right, in here." He pushed open the door to the living room. "Now what is it?"

"You told me David's mother had gone away. Is that true?"

"Of course it's—" He stared at her narrowly. "Has David told you she's dead?"

"Yes."

He groaned. "I thought he'd got over that. It was a stage he went through soon after she left."

"Does he know she's alive?"

"Of course he knows. He's been to stay with her."

"So she does still have some interest in him?"

"Very little. She invited him only at my insistence, and it wasn't a success. But that's no excuse for him lying about her."

"He's not lying," she said, outraged. "He's fantasizing."

"Is there a difference?"

She looked at him for a long, thoughtful moment. "Have you ever had an operation, Mr. Haverill?" she asked at last.

"What on earth—? Yes, I had my appendix out years ago."

"Did they give you an anesthetic?"

"Of course."

"And why? Because the pain would have been too much to bear without help. Well, that's David's situation, too. Can't you imagine the pain of simply being abandoned by the one person in the world who's supposed to put him above everything?"

"He has a father—"

"Fathers aren't the same. It's his mother who's supposed to be there for him, listen to him, cuddle him, defend him—" She stopped abruptly as a sudden rush of emotion threatened to choke her.

"What's the matter?" Giles asked.

"Nothing." She turned away from him, hurriedly brushing her eyes.

"Then why are you crying?"

"I'm not crying," she said firmly.

"Yes, you are." He took her shoulders and turned her toward him, looking closely into her face. "What is it? One minute you were bawling me out in fine style and then something seemed to happen to you. What's wrong?"

His voice had a gentleness she hadn't heard before, and when she met his eyes she found that they were kind. A tremor of apprehension went through her. He must never be allowed to guess the surge of grief that had swept her at the thought of the lost years when she'd hadn't been there to cuddle and defend David, or to listen to his childish confidences.

"It's late," she said hastily. "I'm just tired. The important person is David. The pain is more than he can stand. So he tells himself that his mother's dead, because that way she didn't reject him."

"And that's his anesthetic?" he ventured.

"Right. But at the same time part of him knows she did reject him, and he thinks it's his fault. He told me he was bad. The way he sees it, he must be wicked for his mother to have dumped him without a backward glance."

"*She didn't.*"

Neither of them had seen David in the doorway until his scream alerted them. The next moment he dashed in to confront Melanie. "My mother's dead," he shouted. "She didn't dump me. She didn't, she *didn't.*"

"David—" Giles began in a voice of iron, but the child was beyond hearing him.

"She's dead," he screamed. "She's dead, she's dead, she *dead.*"

He began to hit out, flailing wildly. An ornament went flying. Melanie acted quickly, putting her arms about David and pulling him close to her. He swung around some more, but gradually the message of her enfolding arms got through to him. His words became submerged in a series of violent sobs. Melanie picked him up, torn apart by the feel of the little body shaken with bewildered grief. Giles made a move toward them but she shook her head. He was so surprised at being ordered back that he stopped, staring.

"She's dead, she's dead," David sobbed wildly. "If she wasn't dead—she'd be here—and—and—she'd have come to the concert—and—she'd—she'd have clapped and clapped—she's dead, she is, she *is.*"

The shocked eyes of the two adults met over the child's head. Melanie tried to soothe David with loving murmurs, but he was beyond hearing her. "I want my mommy," he choked, "I want my mommy, *I want my mommy.*"

His arms met tightly behind Melanie's neck. She rested her head on his shining hair, feeling her own tears flow. At last she turned and left the room, carrying David. Giles followed them up the stairs and along the corridor to David's room. He opened the door for her, but she shook her head again, telling him not to follow, but to leave this to her. As she retreated into the bedroom she had a last look at Giles's face, distorted with anguish, but it hardly registered through the need to comfort David.

Giles remained outside for a long time. From inside he could hear his son's sobs, interspersed with Melanie's soothing murmurs. At last he opened the door. In the darkness he could just make out the two figures on the bed, the child clutching the woman around the neck as he wept into her shoulder, the woman with her head bent against him in a timeless gesture of embrace and protection. Giles closed the door. There was an ache in his heart that he couldn't explain.

Melanie was only distantly aware of the door opening and closing. Her whole attention was given up to the little boy in her arms. As she whispered words of love and consolation to him she rocked her body back and forth, unconsciously reassuring him with the rhythm of the cradle. He was gradually falling asleep, but now and then he would murmur, "I want my mommy."

As last there was silence. His head grew heavy on her shoulder, and she realized he'd fallen asleep. "David," she said softly. "David?"

There was no reply. When she was sure he was really asleep, she tightened her arms about him, caressing his hair with her fingers. "It's all right, darling," she breathed. "I'm here. I'm going to stay with you now. Everything's going to be all right."

The warmth of her child's body was unbearably sweet. Her arms had ached for him for so long, and now they held him hungrily. He was hers and she would never let him go again.

She was possessed by a turbulence that was part joy, part anguish. It started in her breast and streamed out through the whole of her body. It was the wall of ice that had enclosed her heart, beginning to crack, the pieces being swept away in a flood of warmth. She was being reborn after years spent in the sleep of death, and like all births it was painful. But it was a good pain, telling her that her heart could feel again.

Her child stirred in her arms and muttered to himself.

"Hush, my darling" she whispered, holding him close. "Mommy's here."

Melanie stayed with David a long time, sometimes dozing but mostly watching over him. She left him in the early hours and went to bed, but she found it hard to sleep, and when the dawn came she got up and went to look in on him. He was still sleeping soundly, and instead of returning to her own room, something impelled her to slip out of the back of the house into the garden.

The sun was just coming up, dispelling the early morning gray, revealing the colors of the flowers. How startling they were, she thought. How blue was the blue, and how green the green! And the chorus of birds overhead, how sweet and loud they sang! They'd all been there for the past eight years, but she hadn't seen or heard them, because she'd been blind and deaf and dead to all feeling. But now the reunion with her child and his need of her had caused a healing within her soul, bringing her senses to life, letting the world reach her again.

It was still chilly from the night and she had on only a thin nightdress and robe, but she wanted to stay here, drinking in the rediscovered beauty of the earth. Impulsively she kicked off her slippers and let her bare feet sink into the dew-damp grass. It felt wonderful.

Just ahead she could hear the sound of a stream bubbling over stones. She made her way toward it and found a little arbor, surrounded by trees, through which the stream ran. It was an enchanted place, where a dreamer might sit for hours in solitary musing, or a place of refuge, to escape from the troubles of the world. Someone certainly seemed to think so, for there, sitting on a fallen log, was Giles. She was about to retreat when something about him arrested her.

He was staring at an object he held. As he turned it, Melanie was astonished to see the last thing she would have expected to find in this man's ruthlessly efficient hands. Incredibly, it was a small teddy bear, a battered, ancient creature with a missing eye, as though some child had loved it to pieces. There was a look of such sadness on Giles's face that she drew in her breath, wondering at the ache in her own breast. She'd felt it before, but only for David. This man had seemed so coldly unsympathetic as to have no feelings worth the name. But now his pain was unmistakable, and it called forth an answer in her newly awakened heart.

He seemed to become aware of her and looked up. "Is David all right?"

"Yes, he's still asleep."

He glanced at her feet. "You'll get pneumonia. Sit down here and dry off," he advised, pulling a handkerchief from his pocket.

There wasn't much room on the log and she had to squeeze against him to mop the dew from her feet. "It feels good to walk barefoot in the wet grass, doesn't it?" he asked. "I used to do it when I was a boy. We lived in this house, and when things went wrong I'd come out here. It was a magic place to me."

"I should think it was," she mused, looking around her. It seemed strange to think of the assured Giles Haverill coming to this pretty little spot for comfort. But obviously he hadn't been assured in those days. He'd been a little boy, much like David.

As though he read her thought, he held up the teddy. "This was his," he said, trying vainly to straighten one of the bear's ears. "It was the first thing I ever bought him, when he was a baby. It was too big for him, of course, but I wanted to get him something at once. He was so tiny and perfect—I'd had my doubts about adopting. I wanted a son of my own, but Zena couldn't have any, so it was the only way. I wasn't sure I could love a child who wasn't mine, but as soon as I saw David—it was just love at first sight." His voice had grown husky. He stopped and laughed self-consciously. "It sounds sentimental, but if only you could have seen how lovely he was as a baby—"

"He must have been delightful," she said in a flat voice to conceal her emotion.

"He was. He had a way of staring at you gravely, without blinking. And then he'd suddenly give a big, beaming smile that would take your breath away. It was—I don't know how to explain it—"

"You don't need to," Melanie said softly.

"It was simply the most wonderful thing that ever happened to me. Once you'd seen that smile—"

Melanie clenched her hands, wondering how much longer she could endure this. "Most men don't go for babies," she forced herself to say lightly.

"I didn't think of myself as a baby lover in those days," he agreed. "But when I saw him, so tiny and defenseless, and needing a home where he was loved—well, he was my son from the first moment. I just went out and bought him a teddy bear. Then I had to go abroad, leaving him here with Zena, and when I saw him again he was six months old. He'd changed so much—they do at that age."

"Yes," she whispered.

"But d'you know, nothing had really changed. He looked different, but he was still my David. It's mysterious and wonderful how love can stay the same over time and distance, and be as strong as ever."

"I know."

Luckily he was too absorbed in his memories to realize that his words had put her on the rack. "When he was old enough to have the teddy bear, he kept it with him all the time, at night, during the day, always. He'd go to sleep cuddling it. I'd creep in sometimes and see him lying there with his cheek against the fur, looking completely happy."

Giles sighed heavily. "He loved me in those days, too. He'd run and put his arms around me, not turn away as he sometimes does now. Why? What went wrong?"

Melanie was silent. She'd got control of herself, but she knew Giles wasn't ready yet to hear what had gone wrong.

"You probably didn't guess this," he said after a moment, "but when I called from the States that night, I hadn't planned to talk to David." He saw her smiling at him. "Yes, of course, you did guess. You maneuvered me into talking with him, didn't you?"

"He was thrilled that you called him."

"Yes. I never thought, you see. I never realized how much more I'd have to be to him when Zena went. I looked in on you after you'd taken him to bed last night. You were cuddling him and you seemed so—perfect together. I'm glad I hired you. I wasn't sure yesterday, but I am today." He hesitated, and she sensed that he was struggling with words that were hard to say. "I should have come to the concert. I'm sorry."

"You'd have been so proud of him." Her increasing knowledge of this man's character made her say, "He didn't make a single mistake."

"That's my boy." He was sunk in thought for a moment. "I was wrong about everything, wasn't I?" he said at last. "I never understood him for a moment."

"As long as you understand him now—"

"But I don't. The only thing I have to hold onto is you. From the first moment, you've known what to say and do. It's strange—as though you and David were connected by an invisible thread."

Melanie tensed as he came so near her secret. But there was nothing but warmth in the smile he turned on her, and her heart gave the same disturbing lurch it had given before.

"Not really so strange," she said. "I just love him, and he knows it."

"But I love him, too. Why can't he—why can't I...? Oh, I don't know what I mean. I suppose he needs a mother more than a father. You're right of course, about him being abandoned by his mother. And it's worse than that, because his natural mother abandoned him, too, and he knows it."

"Is that what you've told him?" Melanie demanded, aghast. "That she *abandoned* him?"

"I didn't need to tell him. He knows. As soon as he knew he was adopted, he asked why his mother had given him away. Naturally we put a good gloss on it, but the brute fact is that she couldn't be bothered with him."

"You don't know that. Maybe she wanted to keep him—"

"Then why didn't she? It's easy enough these days with all the support the state gives. Unmarried mothers don't have to give their babies up unless they want to."

Melanie opened her mouth to rage against this bigoted, easy judgment, but then forced herself to be silent. She was playing for high stakes, too high to be endangered by a flash of temper. Instead she said, with forced calm, "You judge too easily. You might have done her an injustice."

"A woman who could give up her own child?" Giles said scathingly. "How can you do an injustice to someone like that? She must have had a heart of stone."

"But you don't know anything about her. She may have been young and confused. Perhaps she thought she was doing the right thing for the baby. Maybe it broke her heart."

"Nonsense," Giles said impatiently. "Zena actually met her once. She asked her how she could bring herself to give up her own child, and do you know what this woman said? She wanted to play in a rock band, so she dumped her baby. How low can any woman sink?"

Melanie expelled her breath slowly. This new revelation sent her mind reeling. So Zena had told Giles about her visit, but she'd carefully twisted the tale to put her in the worst possible light.

"You've made me realize that she was the start of all David's troubles," Giles said. "She abandoned him first, long before Zena, and that's why he feels he's bad, because two mothers have rejected him. My God, if only I could have that woman here, make her realize the damage she did with her cold-blooded selfishness...."

"Stop it," Melanie cried. He stared at her and she fought to recover herself. "You mustn't talk like that," she said desperately. "He'll hear you—you'll make it worse—he mustn't ever hear you saying—"

"I'm sorry. I'll watch my tongue in future. Come on, don't get upset." He slipped an arm around her shoulders and felt the tremors in her slim body. "You really care about him, don't you?" he asked in a tone of wonder.

"Yes, I do," she said, struggling for composure. "He's such a sad little boy, and he needs love so badly."

Giles's arm tightened. "You shouldn't take things so much to heart," he chided gently.

"Yes, I—I'm being silly, I know—"

He lifted her chin to study her face, wondering at the ravaged look that had suddenly come upon it, and the trace of tears in her eyes. He brushed them away with gentle fingers, only half realizing what he was doing.

His attention was held by the beauty of her eyes, dark with some emotion he didn't understand. "You can't take the whole world's troubles on your shoulders," he said. "I—we—David needs all of you."

Melanie suddenly couldn't breathe. She was intensely aware of his body pressed against hers on the narrow log, the feel of his fingers and the soft brushing of his breath against her face. "Are you all right?" he asked.

"Yes, I—it's just that I didn't sleep much and I—need my breakfast," she finished wildly.

This sudden descent into the prosaic broke the spell. Giles dropped his hand and blinked a little, like a man who'd just come out of a dream. "Yes," he said slowly, "I suppose we should get back inside."

As they mounted the stairs, David was just emerging from his room. He went straight to Melanie and spoke in a determined voice that showed he'd rehearsed this moment. "I told you a fib. Mommy isn't dead. She went away because I was bad."

Giles put his hand on David's shoulder. "You're not bad, old son," he said. "It wasn't your fault." When he found no response in his son's eyes, he repeated, "You're not bad."

"But do you think if I was very, *very* good, Mommy would come back?" David asked simply.

"No," Giles said in a husky voice. "Mommy isn't coming back, and—and it isn't your fault. From now on—we have to look after each other—you and I—and Melanie."

David was regarding Melanie steadily. After a moment he put his hand into hers and gave a gentle squeeze. There was acceptance in the gesture, acceptance that Zena was gone for good, perhaps acceptance of Melanie herself. She couldn't be sure. Her eyes were blurred.

It was Giles who recovered first. "I'm sorry I didn't manage to get to the concert last night," he said. "But won't you give me a performance now, David? Then I won't have missed it."

He saw Melanie's start of joy, but in the child's eyes he read only doubt and confusion.

"You mean—play the piano for you, Daddy?"

"That's right. I'd like to hear what you played last night. Come downstairs, and play it for me."

Like Melanie, Giles recognized the child's talent when he heard him, but the discovery gave him no pleasure. This was his son, *his,* but he echoed too closely the disreputable female who'd tossed him aside to play in a rock band. He'd meant to cut that woman and her influence out of his son's life, offering him instead a wonderful future at the head of a great firm. Yet he, who prided himself on sticking to his guns at all times, had conceded this point. Well, no more. After this the piano would be locked again.

Then his glance fell on David, his eyes alight with an inner glow that might almost have been happiness. A knife seemed to twist inside Giles, and suddenly he was appalled at his own blundering insensitivity.

When the music came to an end, he went and sat beside David on the piano stool, his arm around the little boy's shoulders. "That was fine, son," he said. "Your piano teacher will be pleased. I'll call her today."

He had his reward. David turned and hugged him, speechless with joy. Giles hugged him back, then glanced up to meet Melanie's eyes. *Seeking her approval,* he thought, shocked. *Just like David.* But he couldn't help himself.

Four

———

The following week was enlivened by the final battle with Brenda. Increasingly resentful of Melanie's influence, she'd dropped into the habit of being as rude to her as she dared. Melanie endured the insolence until it turned into abuse of David, at which point she discovered an autocratic streak she hadn't known she possessed, and fired Brenda on the spot.

"You can't fire me," Brenda insisted. "Only Mr. Haverill can do that. I'll tell him what you're really like—"

"Try it," Melanie snapped.

Giles, who'd returned home in time to hear most of the row, backed her up, and within an hour Brenda had departed, clutching three month's notice in lieu of wages.

"So what *are* you really like?" he asked with a grin.

"I'm not sure," she said, bewildered. "I didn't even know I could act like that."

"Neither did I. To think you dared call *me* overbearing!"

She shared his laughter. The next moment David had come running downstairs to greet his father and the moment passed.

Melanie interviewed a couple of women for the cooking and cleaning. Neither was hired until they'd met David and liked him. One of them, Mrs. Wade, admitted nervously that her daughter Sylvia would sometimes have to come with her. Sylvia turned out to be a shrewish seven-year-old who promptly challenged David to see who could stick their tongue out the farthest. Hearing their shrieks of laughter, Melanie engaged Sylvia's mother without delay.

The two cleaners took shifts, neither staying overnight, and when David had gone to bed, Melanie had the house to herself until Giles's return. Coming home late one evening, he found her curled up on the sofa. She'd been watching television when she fell into a doze, and awoke to find him peering at her with a quizzical half smile.

Caught unaware, she had no defense against the sudden fast beating of her heart. At their first meeting she'd told him that, like himself, she was armored against attraction. She'd believed it. But the breaking down of her barriers had left her open to a world of new sensations, and now she received the full impact of his blazing male vitality. She took an unsteady breath. "Hello," she said.

"Hello, sleepyhead. Has he tired you out?"

"Mmm. We've been playing pirates." She brushed back her hair which had tumbled over her face as she slept, and yawned. When she tried to get up, her cramped body could hardly move. Giles took her hands and pulled her to her feet, steadying her as her legs protested. "Thanks," she said breathlessly, and drew quickly away from him.

"Have supper with me," he said.

"Lovely. I'm famished."

He refused to let her help except in minor ways. "You'd be amazed how handy I am with a freezer and a microwave," he said with a self-deprecating grin.

Since the concert their relationship had undergone a subtle change, which the Brenda incident had symbolized. Giles had accepted Melanie as an expert where David was concerned, and expertise was something he respected. Melanie's view of him had been irrevocably altered when she'd heard him speak of his love for the infant David in terms that echoed her own feelings. It had been easier to think of him as an unfeeling man who was her enemy. The discovery that he loved her child as much as she did threw her into a confusion from which she had not yet recovered.

They sat in the kitchen to eat pizza, washed down with red wine, and when he'd taken the edge off his hunger, he asked, "Why pirates?"

"I started telling him about my childhood. We lived near a lake, so everyone learned to sail. We'd form gangs, pirates and buccaneers." She gave a chuckle. "We flew the Jolly Roger, and made each other walk the plank. There was an island where we used to chase and hide, and hunt for buried treasure."

"How old are you?" Giles asked with a grin.

"Twenty-five. Why?"

"For a moment, there, you looked about ten. It's good to see you smiling for once. You were so tense and grim when you came here for your interview."

"I wasn't grim," she said, laughing.

"You should have seen yourself, clammed up as though you were keeping the lid on a pressure cooker. I've seen that look only once before. It was on the face of a man who'd deceived me into signing a contract by concealing some vital information, and all through the signing he was on edge in case I discovered his secret. I don't know why you should make me think of that, because he was a cheat and you're the most honest person I've ever known."

Her pulses were racing at the risk that had grown suddenly close, but luckily he was too absorbed by what he was saying to notice. "I've watched you with David, and I know that it was our lucky day when you came here. I'm not often fooled, Melanie, and never by the same person twice. When I discovered what that man had done—well, let's just say that he's in jail now, brooding over his mistake." Giles made a noise of impatience. "Listen to me, bringing everything back to business, and I promised myself I wouldn't do that tonight. Let me drink to you, for the change you've caused in my home—the change in David, and in me, if I'm honest."

"What an admission," she said lightly, to cover her unease. Giles's trust gave her a pang of guilt about her deception. It had been forced on her, but still...

"It *is* a considerable admission," Giles said, grinning. "More than you know. I'm a prickly customer."

"I'd never have guessed." They laughed together. To her alarm Melanie felt a surge of warm pleasure go through her. Such feelings were dangerous and forbidden, but she was too inexperienced in the game of attraction to be able to counter them.

Playing for safety, she changed the subject. "There's still so much I don't know about David. How long have you been back from Australia?"

She knew at once that she'd made a mistake. Giles looked at her in surprise. "How did you know we'd been to Australia? Surely David didn't tell you? He was only two when we left there."

"Ah—no, not David," she said, struggling to recover from her slip. "It must have been in the school records."

"Odd. I don't remember telling them, but I suppose I must have done. We went there so that I could establish a branch of my father's firm. Funny that I should have mentioned Australia and not Italy, where we went afterward. We came back when my father died suddenly. I'd counted on several more years abroad so that David could get used to the countries where we operate."

"You're very sure that David will go into the firm?"

"Of course. He's a Haverill."

"But he isn't. He's adopted."

"He's my son, as much as if I was his biological father. I don't do anything by halves, Melanie."

No, she thought. You didn't take half measures when you revenged yourself on that man. You don't hate in half measure, or love...

She caught herself up, wondering why her thoughts were so hard to control these days.

"I just meant that you should let him be a little boy before he has to think about the future," she said. "Have you noticed the walls of his bedroom? Empty, except for a couple of tasteful pictures."

"Is that so bad?"

"It's terrible. A boy of eight doesn't want good taste. He wants acid drop colors and pictures of pop stars and characters from computer games. What did you have on the wall when you were eight?"

Giles grinned suddenly. "Captain Hero and his Daredevil Crew."

"Well, there you are then. Actually David knows about Captain Hero because he's on a computer game and we play it together."

"I bought him that computer as an educational asset," Giles protested, not very seriously.

"Well, it's educating me at the moment. I'm learning a lot about David from the way he plays. He's got a gentle streak that I daresay you'd disapprove of. He always hesitates before going in for the kill." She added ironically, "You'll have to cure that if he's going to run the firm."

He leaned back in his chair and regarded her humorously. "Are you getting at me?"

"Do you think I am?" she asked lightly.

"I think you've been getting at me in one way or another since the day you arrived."

She took a deep breath. "Mr. Haverill—"

"I think you might call me Giles by now."

"Giles—have you given any thought to taking David away on a vacation?"

He frowned. "He ought to have one, of course, but I'm up to my ears in work. The two of you could—no, I made that mistake before, didn't I?"

"Surely you've got a good deputy who could handle things for a couple of weeks?"

He regarded her wryly. "I feel sure you've got something planned."

"Not exactly planned. But talking about pirates made David wish he could sail. Do you know how to sail?"

"A little. When we were in Italy I did business with a man who owned a sailing center on Lake Garda. It was called Blue Water, and it was a marvelous place. I could give him a call."

"That will mean the world to David. If only you knew—the chance to spend some time alone with you—"

"But you'll be there?" he asked sharply.

"Oh, yes, but it's your attention he wants. Give him all of it, Giles, please."

Her eyes were fixed on him, shining, eager. For the hundredth time he tried to analyze the change that had come over her recently, but as always it eluded him. There was a new softness about her, a sympathy that sometimes seemed to be for him, as well as David. In the bleak loneliness of his life that sympathy was a sweet balm. But there was more, a mystery that increasingly intrigued him. Perhaps in Italy he would find the clue.

From then on Giles began to notice that whenever he received a phone call David would linger within earshot, with an air of tension. He didn't discover why until the day before they were due to leave, when he received a call from Jack Taggen, a source of valuable tips.

"Van Lyman's going to be in town," Taggen said.

Giles made a sound of triumph at the name of the man he'd been eager to contact. "When will he be here?"

"Next week. Thursday and Friday."

"Thursday and Fri..." He realized that both David and Melanie were watching him. Various often-used speeches, all of them starting with "I'm sorry, David, but—'' flickered through his head, only to be instantly dismissed. He turned back to Taggen. "That's a pity," he said. "I shall be away then."

"Surely you can cancel it?" Taggen demanded. "This man's business is worth millions."

Suddenly Giles knew that this was why David had been holding himself tense every time the telephone rang. He was waiting for his father to disappoint him. *Expecting* it.

"Sorry," he told Taggen. "I'm taking my son on vacation, and we want no interruptions."

He barely heard the gasp of astonishment from the other end. He was watching David's face, and the look of disbelieving wonder that shone from it smote him to the heart. Then, much against his will, he glanced at Melanie. It was her smile and nod of approval that completed the moment for him, and this knowledge made him so annoyed with himself that he almost slammed down the phone.

The time before the holiday passed in a whirlwind of activity. Giles handed Melanie his gold card and commanded her to "fill the gaps," which she took to mean the gaps in their vacation equipment. But when she'd fitted David out in clothes suitable for two weeks of sun and sailing, she found it meant much more.

"You were supposed to get things for yourself as well," Giles told her. "Do it in style."

She felt like Cinderella preparing for the ball. Her modest earnings had never bought her the kind of things she could afford now, and she gave herself up to the pleasure of buying good clothes, topped off with anticipation of a perfect two weeks. The first time she went on one of these expeditions she took David with her, but this proved a definite failure, as a more experienced mother could have warned her. David's idea of a good time didn't include hanging around changing rooms in clothing stores, and after that she left him with Mrs. Wade and Sylvia before sallying forth to enjoy herself.

With one day to go she made a last trip to buy forgotten odds and ends, and finished the day exhausted but happy in a small tea shop. While she waited for her tea to arrive, she examined the gift she'd bought for David and smiled as she thought how he would enjoy it.

"Mind if I sit down?"

Smiling mechanically, Melanie looked up. Then she froze and the smile died from her face, to be replaced by a look of horror as a man drew out a chair and sat down opposite her. "Hello, Melanie," he said.

At last she found her voice. "Oliver," she whispered. "Oh, I don't believe it. *Oliver.*"

But it was true. The nightmare was real. This was the man she'd once thought she loved, there in the flesh.

"Still recognize me? I'd have known you anywhere," he said, regarding her through narrowed eyes. "As soon as I saw you I said, 'Oliver, my lad, that's her all right.''

She remembered his habit of quoting what he'd said to himself, and how it had struck a jarring note, even in the days of her infatuation. Looking at him now she wondered how she could ever have loved him. The weakness of his mouth, which she'd barely noticed then, was more pronounced. Something in his eyes, which had looked like shrewdness years ago, now merely seemed sly, and he had a general air of seediness.

"Done well for yourself, haven't you?" he went on saying. "Nice clothes, posh house."

"How do you know where I live?" she asked, trying to ignore a chill that was running up her spine.

"I've been watching you for the last few days, haven't I? And I'm impressed. Always one to land on her feet, that's my Melanie."

"I'm not your Melanie," she said, recovering her composure. "I was once, but you didn't want to know."

"If I'd known how you were going to turn out I might have wanted to."

"Oliver, why rake over the past?" she asked wearily. "It's dead. So are the people we were then. I don't know what made you watch me, or how you knew where to watch, but does it really matter?"

"It could. Finding you was the kind of lucky fall of the dice that convinces me things are going my way at last. I've had a lot of bad luck. I borrowed some money from a firm I was working in—just borrowed. I'd have paid it back. But then Giles Haverill decided to take the firm over, and while he was looking through the books he discovered my little sleight of hand. The long and the short of it was that I was out of a job, and I haven't been able to get a decent one since. I came here, because I reckon I owe something to Mr. Giles Haverill. So I start watching his house, and who should come out, but my ladylove—"

"I'm not your ladylove," she said passionately. "Don't ever call me that again. I want nothing more to do with you."

"Don't be so hasty. You don't know what I'm going to say. I've been doing some investigating, and I've discovered a few very interesting facts. I know you're employed to look after Haverill's adopted son. Tell me, does he know you're David's real mother?''

The question caught her by surprise, jerking a gasp from her before she could control it. Oliver's cunning little eyes were on her, gauging every tiny reaction. But she did her best. "You're talking nonsense," she said, rallying. "I don't know where you got such a crazy idea from—"

For answer he tossed a photograph onto the table in front of her. It showed a fair-haired boy of about eight, wearing a striped sweater. Melanie seized it up with a shaking hand. "How did you get David's pic—no, it's not David," she stammered.

"That's right. It's a snapshot of my younger brother, Phil, taken years ago. But it's the image of David, isn't it? Phil got his looks from our dad—and *he* was grand-father to David. Blood will out. That's my son you're looking after. Yours and mine."

If he said any more she felt she would be sick. "Don't talk about David as your son," she flung at him. "You were never a father to him."

"And you were never a mother," he retorted with a complacency that made her want to hit him. "You got rid of him fast enough."

"It didn't—it was for his sake—I loved him—"

"So that's why you took this job, to be with him?" Oliver asked, apparently sympathetic.

"Yes. I just wanted—"

"You wanted your son. Is Haverill going to give him to you?"

"Of course not. It's not like that."

"So what is it like? Suppose his wife comes back, or he marries someone else. What happens to you then?

You want that kid back, don't you? And I'm here to show you how to do it.''

She pulled herself together. "What do you mean?" she demanded, looking him in the eye. Her heart was hammering.

"I mean that I want him, too. That'll teach Mr. Nosey Parker Haverill to stick his nose in.''

"You're mad," she said scornfully. "He was legally adopted. No court will give him to you.''

"But it might give him to you and me together. We can go to that Braddock woman—oh, yes, I know all about her. She wants David to have a proper home, with two parents. Well, *we're* his natural parents. I think Mrs. Braddock would be interested in talking to us.'' He watched her face as this registered. "Do you realize what I mean?" he said softly. "You can have David back.''

For a moment the vision dazzled her. Herself and David, together forever. Mother and son, as nature had made them.

Then the vision wavered slightly. The look of eagerness on David's face was for Giles as much as herself. For all the tensions and misunderstandings between them, the little boy adored the man he thought of as a father, and his anguish would be complete if they were parted.

But he would forget, whispered the tempter. Children are resilient. When he knew that his real mother had come for him, surely that would make him happy?

"You want him back, I know you do," Oliver said softly. "This is your chance." He gave a short laugh. "And *my* chance to make Haverill very, very sorry.''

But he'd overreached himself. His sneering words dispelled the lovely vision. Suddenly Giles was there in her mind, as she'd seen him in the garden, riven with sadness as he told her how deeply he loved his little son. What Oliver was proposing would destroy Giles, and David, too. Now momentary weakness was swept away by a flash of clarity that showed her in a stark and terrible light what she'd been tempted to do. To tear her child away from the one person who represented safety in his turbulent world would be an act of selfish cruelty. And she couldn't do it.

Now she felt as if she were made of pure ice. "Forget it," she said bluntly. "I won't help you, Oliver."

"Don't be a fool," he snapped. "Of course you'll help me. You want David back."

"Not at the cost of breaking his heart, and breaking Giles's heart."

Oliver swore impatiently. "Load of sentimental nonsense. Hearts mend. He's our kid and I want him."

"You won't get him through me."

"For Pete's sake, be reasonable. It's in your interests as much as mine."

"My interests." She mused over the words. "My interests don't seem so important anymore. Not important enough to injure my son."

"But I tell you we'd be doing him a good turn, giving him his rightful parents—"

"I can't think of anything worse than giving him you as a father," she said coldly. "I'll have nothing to do with this idea, and that's final."

His face took on an ugly look. "Aiming for a bigger prize, eh?" he said, sneering. "Think you can land Haverill himself? Much chance you stand."

"Get out, Oliver. Get out of my life and don't come around me again."

"Oh, I'll be back. You'll see sense in the end."

"You expect me to change my mind? Not in a million years."

"You're forgetting about that picture of Phil," Oliver said nastily. "When I produce it, do you really think you can deny that I'm David's father?"

Melanie made a desperate throw of the dice. "I can do better than that. *I can deny that I'm his mother.* See how much good your picture does you then. You can't touch Giles or David without my help, Oliver, and you'll never have it. *Never.*"

She rose to leave. Oliver made a grab for her but she twisted away. He tried again, and in the scuffle a pot of hot tea ended up all over him. As he mopped himself down, cursing loudly, Melanie made her escape. When she ran to the car and got in, at first she could hardly put the key in the ignition, her hands were shaking so badly. But the thought that he might follow her gave her the strength to drive home.

She was filled with horror at the knowledge that this revolting, conniving creature knew where she lived, where David lived. The thought of him plotting and scheming to hurt them drove her into the house, calling David's name. There was no reply, and she stood listening to the silent house, a prey to nameless terrors.

Then the sound of a child's chuckle reached her from the garden. She hurried out but still there was no sign of David. The chuckle came again, and this time she followed it to the special place by the stream where she'd once seen Giles. He was there now, but this time David was with him. They were absorbed in looking into the water at something Giles was showing his son, and Melanie had a moment to watch them without being seen. It was the first time she'd seen them so natural and happy in each other's company, and a hand seemed to clutch her heart as she thought of the threat hanging over them.

"I won't let him," she murmured to herself. "I'll do whatever I have to to protect them."

Giles looked up and smiled as he saw her. "So you're back. Why, what's the matter? You're as white as a sheet." He laid a gentle hand on her arm and smiled in the way that meant so much to her these days. "What is it?" he asked again.

"Nothing—nothing—" she said, trying to marshal her thoughts. "It's just been a tiring day."

"Melanie, Melanie, look what I've got," David called. He held up something long and slimy that he'd pulled from the stream.

"Yuk!" she said involuntarily.

"I warned you she wouldn't like it," Giles told him. "Women don't understand these things." He turned back to her. "You're really looking pale. You need that vacation."

"Yes, I do. I'm so glad that we're going away tomorrow."

Five

Reaching Blue Water was like reaching paradise. The warm sun blessed them as they left the plane, and the waters of the lake glinted invitingly. The biggest of the Italian lakes, Garda was nearly forty miles long, by twenty miles at its widest point. "It's like being by the sea," David said excitedly. "You can't see the other side."

The lake was alive with Windsurfers and sailors, and Blue Water itself was situated on one of the most glorious sandy beaches Melanie had ever seen. Giles had booked the best chalet, with three bedrooms, a veranda and a magnificent view over the lake. "Can we go swimming *now?*" David pleaded as soon as they were inside.

"Wait till we've unpacked, son," Giles said. "We don't know where the swimsuits are yet."

"Of course we do," Melanie told him, diving into her hand luggage. "I kept them apart on purpose."

"I give in. We'll go swimming now."

In the end she was last out of her room, while Giles and David, suitably attired, stood outside her door singing, 'Why are we waiting?' Giles's baritone blending with David's sweet soprano.

"I'm coming, I'm coming," she yelped. The next instant she was out, laughing and protesting as David jumped on her.

Giles was glad that the two of them were absorbed in each other. It gave him a moment to recover from his shock at the sight of her. He'd always known she had a slim, beautiful figure, but he'd never realized its full glory until he saw her in her swimming suit. It was a simple, black one-piece that made no attempt to be seductive, but nothing could disguise her tiny waist, full breasts and long, elegant legs. He knew an intense desire to reach out and touch her, but luckily the presence of his son restrained him, and by the time they'd finished romping he had himself under control again.

In the water the black suit turned her into a sleek, lovely seal, twisting this way and that as she laughed and played with David, as untroubled as a child herself. Giles silently blessed her for making him do this, for already he was beginning to feel good.

As they came out of the water there was a shout of "Melanie—hey, Melanie."

She looked around and her face broke into a smile at the sight of a family coming along the beach waving to her. "It's the Fraynes," she told Giles. "I looked after the children once. That's George and Celia, the parents, and the tall, good-looking young man is Jack, Celia's brother."

It hadn't seemed to Giles that Jack was notably good-looking and he merely grunted.

"Fancy finding you here," George yelled, enfolding her in a bear hug. He was a grizzled, middle-aged man with a loud voice and a huge smile. Melanie made the introductions and within a few minutes the two parties had joined up. David was shy at first, but his reserve soon broke down under the friendliness of the Frayne children.

"Look at him," she murmured to Giles as the children chased each other. "That's just what he needs."

"And he's forgotten his father," Giles observed with a grin. "Although it was supposed to be my company he wanted."

"He needs to know you're here whether he's with you or not. He'd mind fast enough if you weren't here."

He laughed. He was feeling cheerful and relaxed. "I see. Be around but stay in the background in case of need—like a doorknob."

She looked at him earnestly. "But that's exactly it. Don't you see? That's what parents are for."

"I'm beginning to see." His voice grew casual. "You must know the family very well."

"Well, I lived with them for three months. Celia was in hospital and George spent a lot of time with her, so Jack and I coped with the children together." She laughed. "You wouldn't think it to look at those Adonis looks and all that charm, but Jack's terrific with children."

"It hadn't struck me that he was especially charming," Giles said with a slight edge on his voice.

Melanie chuckled. "No, men don't see it. But women do. Jack's broken more hearts in his time than—*David*, be careful! Don't trip Annie up. She's only little."

"Broken more hearts?" Giles persisted.

"Sorry?"

"You were telling me about Jack. It seems that no woman is immune."

"I think we'd better go over there," Melanie said, her eyes on the children. "It's turning into roughhousing."

She scampered away across the sand, leaving Giles to follow in her wake. He felt vaguely unsettled, as though the sun had inexplicably gone in.

They spent the next few days with the Fraynes, fooling around on the *Margarita,* the yacht the family had hired, and taking excursions across the lake. As Melanie had said, David didn't need the adults' constant attention so much as the reassurance that they were there. He would often look up to check their presence before returning happily to a melee with the other children.

His preoccupation with his new friends gave Melanie the chance to renew her acquaintance with Jack, whom she'd once regarded as a kind of kid brother. "No more music?" he asked one day as they lazed in the sun.

"No, I've given that up. I'm happy looking after David." She kept her voice casual. Jack knew nothing about her lost child, still less that she'd found him again.

"A baby-sitter! You! I remember seeing you play in the band, all black leather and wiggling hips."

"Shh!" she admonished him. "My boss doesn't know about my colorful past."

"Wouldn't approve, huh? What happened to his wife?"

"She left."

"Without taking the kid? Poor little soul." Jack looked at her suddenly. "Is her name Zena?"

"Yes. How did you know?"

"I overheard him on the phone to her yesterday."

"What? Are you sure?"

"He definitely said 'Zena,' and then 'Please listen to me.' Perhaps he's trying to get her back."

"I don't think so," Melanie said in a hollow voice.

"Well, shouldn't he be making the effort? She may not have been much good, but she's David's *mother*. Best thing all round if they get back together. Hey, you kids! Cut it out!" He yelled, ducking a spray that had drenched him, and in the mayhem that followed, Melanie managed to avoid further discussion.

"You're very quiet," Giles said as they went home that evening.

"Am I? I'm just tired, I guess."

"It seemed to me that you went quiet suddenly while you were talking to Jack. Like a light that had gone out. What's the matter, Melanie?"

"Nothing. You're imagining things."

If only she could be alone to come to terms with the dreadful possibility Jack had opened up. Zena might return, and she would lose David again. Not only that— her mind fought shy of the thought, but it wouldn't be kept out—she would lose Giles.

Since that morning in the garden, when she'd looked at him and known that her heart had awoken, not only to sight and sounds, but feelings, too, she'd been aware of the growing bond between them. She hadn't given it a name, although she was sure it wasn't love. It was more a kind of camaraderie and understated affection, and it was very sweet to her.

She'd discovered that the stern, tense man of the early days could laugh, and that there was pleasure in the rich sound. Sometimes they laughed together, and when their eyes met, the happiness that suffused her made her want to sing. When he held her, to steady her against a rocking boat, the warmth and firmness of his hands gave her a start of pleasure and made her wish he would draw her against him.

But now she'd been shown a future in which it might all be taken away, and the pain in her heart was shocking.

When she kissed David good-night, he put his arms about her neck. "Why are you crying?" he whispered.

"I'm not," she said huskily.

The door clicked behind her. "Daddy, why is Melanie crying? Have you been unkind to her?"

"Not that I know of," Giles replied. He touched her gently. "What's the matter, Melanie?"

"Nothing. The two of you are being absurd. I'll go away so that you can say good-night." She fled the room, and by the time Giles emerged she had herself under control again.

"David is really loving this vacation, isn't he?" she said brightly.

He closed David's door behind him. "Yes, and I can't tell you how grateful I am to you for suggesting it. It's going to make it easier for me to tell him something."

"Yes?" she said. Her heart was hammering as her nightmare started to come true.

"I called Zena yesterday. I've been thinking for some time that—well, Zena and I—"

"Daddy." David's voice interrupted him.

"I'll be back in a moment," Giles said, heading for his son's room.

But as soon as he was gone, Melanie fled the chalet. She wasn't ready to hear what was coming next. It was quiet along the darkening shore and she could run without attracting attention. This was what Oliver had warned her about, for his own purposes. Zena would return and she would lose David again. She was facing a parting even more painful than the last.

She slowed as another thought occurred to her. How long would Zena stay? She was so clearly an indifferent mother that even now if Melanie joined forces with Oliver—

Temptation racked her. She stood irresolute for a long time, until at last, with despair, she recognized what she must do. *"No,"* she cried to the uncaring sky. "I won't do it. I couldn't do that to David. I couldn't—I couldn't..."

She began to run again, as fast as she could, as though trying to outstrip her demons. But they dogged her relentlessly, and it took all her courage to turn and go back to the chalet, knowing what was awaiting her there. Dawn was breaking as she arrived, and Giles was waiting at the door. "Where did you get to?" he asked. "I was worried."

"I'm sorry. I needed a run."

"Just like that? Without any warning? You look very pale."

"That's the effect of being up all night." To distract him, she said, "I'm dying for a cup of tea."

He made her some, and as they drank it, he said, "How about the three of us taking a little boat out together today? If you feel up to it."

"What were you going to tell me last night—about you and Zena?"

"Oh, that? The thing is that for David's sake I thought Zena and I should try to get back together. In fact I actually asked her to try. It went against the grain, because whatever love we had is dead, but David—"

He seemed to have trouble going on. Melanie gripped the side of her chair. "And?" she managed to say.

"Well, the fact is—Zena's getting married again today. Of course that's the end of any idea of reconciliation, and my problem was how to tell him."

She stared at him. "Zena—getting married—?"

"To the fellow she left me for. Actually I was worrying about nothing. After you left last night I simply told David, and you know what? He wasn't upset. He just said, 'But we've got Melanie, haven't we?' I told him we had and—Melanie?"

"I'm fine," she said quickly. "I'm just tired from all that walking." She had to get away from him. If she stayed, she was going to burst into tears from some emotion she was afraid to examine too closely just now. "I'll lie down for a while."

"Not for too long. Look at the sun coming up. It's going to be a glorious day."

"Yes, it is," she said unsteadily. "A glorious, glorious day."

Ridiculous! Absurd! To be so happy because Zena was out of Giles's life! Out of David's life, too—that was the part that really counted, she reminded herself. But it was hard to remember that when Giles was there in front of her, his lean, hard-muscled body glistening with water, his skin bronzed by the sun.

The boat lurched and she was thrown against him, felt his bare legs next to hers, and the swift coming and going of her breath. She wondered if her consciousness of him as a man was reflected in her face, then realized that his breath, too, was coming raggedly.

They pulled the boat into shore and had lunch at a lakeside café. Melanie swung a light scarf around her shoulders to protect them from the blazing sun, and sat happily watching David and Giles. They seemed more at ease with each other here, as though the unfamiliar surroundings had made them relax. Soon they would return home, and the problems of everyday life would resurface, but there was time to worry about that later. For now it was enough to see them laughing and enjoying each other's company.

"I suppose we should go back to the chalet," she said as the sun began to sink in the sky. She spoke reluctantly.

"I suppose we should," Giles responded, sounding no more keen.

"Can I take the tiller?" David begged.

Giles ruffled his hair. "That's right, son. You do the work and let us relax."

If they didn't entirely relax, they gave a good imitation of it, letting David feel he was in charge of the boat. Giles watched him with pride, and when they finally tied up he rested a fond hand on the boy's shoulder, earning a beaming smile.

They stopped to hail Miss Witney, one of a group of elderly ladies who'd just moved into the next chalet. She touched Melanie lightly on the arm. "You must be very proud of your son," she said.

"My—?" Melanie stared at her wildly, wondering how this stranger came to know her secret.

"Isn't he your son?"

"He's mine," Giles said, smiling at her. "Melanie helps me look after him."

"Oh, dear, I do beg your pardon. It's just that the three of you look like such a perfect family."

Giles looked pleased. "Yes, I suppose we do."

"And with his hair being the same color as yours—"
Miss Witney said to Melanie.

"So it is!" Giles exclaimed. "D'you know, I'd never
noticed that before."

"Nonsense!" Melanie said in alarm. "We both have
fair hair. So do lots of people. It just looks the same in
this brilliant sun. Excuse me, I must have left my scarf
in the boat."

But when she searched the boat there was no sign of
her scarf. "Did you see it?" she asked Giles, when she
returned to the chalet."

"You probably left it at the café."

"No, I didn't. I remember putting it on as we left."

He shrugged. "Then it probably fell into the water.
Now, what are we going to have for supper?"

The day after they arrived, Melanie had discovered
Giles's guilty secret.

"Portable computer and fax machine, hmm?" she
said, eyeing him mischievously.

"Look," he said hurriedly, with a nervous eye on
David's door, "I just can't spend two weeks completely out of touch, but I promise to wait until he's
asleep." He gave a rueful grin that was half a plea.
"Don't give me away."

"All right, I won't."

He was as good as his word, always being there for
David during the day, and working in secret at night.
Luckily David slept like a top, exhausted by his non-
stop activities, and Giles escaped detection.

Melanie emerged from David's room one evening,
quietly shutting the door behind her. "Is he asleep?"
Giles asked.

"Dead to the world." She chuckled. "Now you'll be able to get to work."

"It can wait until we've had supper."

"Actually, would you mind if I went out? Jack's asked me to have a meal with him."

"Fine," he said shortly.

"Are you sure?" she looked at him, puzzled by an edge in his voice.

"I said it's fine. Go along and enjoy yourself."

"I won't go if it's going to make you snap at me."

He tried to pull himself together. It was ridiculous to feel this sudden malaise just because she wanted a few hours off. "I wasn't aware that I was snapping."

"Well, you were."

"It's just that when you came for an interview, this was the kind of thing you promised me wouldn't happen."

"Hold on. I promised I wouldn't get married. I never said I wouldn't go out for a meal with an old friend."

"A meal with a friend can be the precursor to getting married," he retorted. He knew he was being irrational but he couldn't stop himself. And what in heaven had made him use a stuffy word like precursor?

"It's going to be a pleasant evening, chatting about old times," Melanie said firmly. "So there's no need for you to act like Hamlet when he'd just seen the ghost."

He rubbed his eyes. "Don't take any notice of me, Melanie. All this unaccustomed exercise has left me feeling worn-out. Go and have a great time."

She vanished into her room and he was left feeling thoroughly dissatisfied with everything, but mostly with himself. He knew he couldn't have handled it worse if he'd tried. The fact was that the discovery that she had interests outside himself and David had filled him with sheer outrage. And with a kind of fear.

When she emerged half an hour later, made-up and wearing a pretty dress, he held his tongue, but something knotted in his stomach. He bid her goodbye and watched her leave calmly enough, but his heart was in turmoil. For heaven's sake, he argued with himself, it's the first evening she's had off since she started working for you. She didn't know that young man was going to be here.

Or did she?

Suddenly the whole arrangement took on the aspect of a sinister plot. She'd tricked him into this vacation so that she could be with her 'Adonis.' She'd even tricked him into paying for the dress she was wearing to entice her lover. For several moments Giles's world was filled with lurid colors that threw strange and fearful shadows. Then his common sense returned. "I'm getting paranoid," he muttered. "Of course she didn't plan it."

But he felt shaken. He was a severely practical man, never troubled by imaginings, yet for a while his fancies had been more real than reality. He rubbed his eyes, trying to force himself back to normal, wondering what was happening to him.

He snatched up the phone, called New York and gave his underlings a blistering ten minutes that made them run around. When he'd finished, his son's door opened, and a sleepy figure stood there, rubbing his eyes. "Where's Melanie?" David asked.

"She's gone out for a walk."

"I'm thirsty."

Giles got some milk from the kitchen, and they had a glass each. "When will she be coming back?" David wanted to know.

"Later this evening."

"Promise?"

"Yes, son," Giles said gently. "I promise. She'll come in and say good-night to you."

David allowed himself to be led back to bed and tucked in. The curtains were open a crack and Giles went to close them. In the shining moonlight he could make out two figures on the shore. Melanie was leaning back against a tree, looking up and laughing at her companion, whose head seemed to Giles to be unnecessarily close. As he watched, they began to walk on, Jack's arm around her shoulder. Giles strained to see more, but they'd vanished into shadow.

"Will she be back very soon?" David murmured.

"Go to sleep, son," Giles said heavily,

Jack Frayne made one last effort. "You know, you're even lovelier than you were two years ago," he murmured.

Melanie laughed directly up into his face. "Come on, Jack, you know I can't keep a straight face when you talk like that. Tonight was going to be just friendly. You gave me your word."

"Don't worry. I haven't forgotten what happened the only time I came on strong with you. My face was tingling for a week afterward."

"It's been a lovely evening. Let's leave it at that."

He looked at her closely. "You know, you've changed. You're more alive than when I knew you."

"Well—people do change."

"It's not Haverill, is it?"

"Of course not," she said too quickly.

"Oh, I see," he said in a knowing voice.

"You don't see anything, and I'd like to go back."

She let herself quietly into the chalet, but Giles was up and sitting at his computer. "You took your time," he grumbled. "I didn't know you meant to be out so late."

"Has David—?"

"David's been asking for you. He was scared that you might not come back."

Melanie slipped into David's room. His eyes were open and he greeted her sleepily, but when she kissed him and pulled up the sheet he fell asleep at once. "Nothing to worry about," she said, returning to Giles.

"Good. Did you have a nice time?"

"Yes, lovely. We went dancing, and—"

"It was a polite inquiry. I don't need to hear all the details," he interrupted her.

"In that case I'll go to bed," she said crossly. "Good night."

"Good night."

Six

Melanie awoke several hours later to find the sun high in the sky. Puzzled, she bounded out of bed and looked into David's room, but it was empty. "David's gone," she said, hurrying out to Giles.

"He's been gone an hour. The Fraynes have taken a whole party of kids for a sail on the *Margarita,* so I said he could go. I don't have any worries about him with them."

"No, of course not. But I could have gone with him."

"I didn't like to disturb you," he said, turning his head away and searching for something, lest she suspect how firmly he'd vetoed her spending a day on the same boat as Jack Frayne.

"So now you've got a whole day to get on with 'business,'" Melanie said with a chuckle.

"Business? Oh, yes, business. What are you going to do?"

"Have a swim."

"D'you know," he said with an air of discovery, "I might just drop everything and come with you."

"Drop everything?" she mocked him lightly. "You?"

He grinned. "Come on."

The sun seemed to have come out especially for them as they raced along the pier and dived into the water. Melanie was a strong swimmer, and Giles had to work to keep up with her as she headed out for deep water. It occurred to him that he spent too much time in stuffy offices and not enough time swimming with mermaids.

At last Melanie paused and turned on her back, letting her fair hair splay out in the water. "Mmm," she said blissfully, letting the sun play on her wet limbs. Her eyes were half-closed, but she was aware of him beside her, reaching out to touch her shoulder. At the last second she ducked under water, writhing and spinning away from him. He called her name, looking around him with the beginnings of alarm, but then her head broke the surface some yards away. "Catch me," she called, stroking strongly back to shore.

He plunged after her, catching her as they reached land and chasing her up the beach. "Wretch," he said. "Giving me a scare like that."

She laughed at him and he seized her shoulders, giving her a little shake. "Melanie!"

He felt as if he'd never truly seen her before. With her strong, golden limbs and tumbling fair hair she might have been a Viking maid, a conquering warrior lass. He wasn't a poetical man, but the images that chased through his head were all of strength tempered by softness and beauty, and they left him confused. A sudden surge of self-consciousness made him take his hands from her and say, "I'm hungry."

They dried off and found a fish restaurant where they could sit out in the sun. Melanie leaned back and watched him through half-closed eyes, trying not to be impressed by his broad, muscular shoulders, lean hips and powerful thighs. Only a short time ago she could have regarded him without disturbance, protected by the ice in which she'd lived for so long. But with the ice melted and every sense sharpened, she was fully alive to his vital masculine presence. It was dangerous but she couldn't shut him out.

When he'd seized hold of her on the beach she'd thought for a moment that he might kiss her. She'd both dreaded and wanted that kiss. It would be foolish, unwise, an awkward complication. All these sensible thoughts presented themselves in good order, but the tingling eagerness in her flesh made a nonsense of them. The sight of him now, his big body thrown back in the sun, his long legs stretched out, the whole of him a study in careless power, filled her with a sense of excitement. It was so long since she'd known that feeling, and last time it had ended in disaster, but this man was different....

He looked up, and as soon as he met her eyes she was suffused by warmth. She could feel the color spreading over her breasts and upward to her face, revealing everything she would have been wiser to deny. Then he looked away quickly, consulting the menu, and the moment might never have been, except that his voice wasn't quite steady.

The food was served, and as they started to eat, the atmosphere became more relaxed. "Sorry I was such a bear last night," he said. "I've grown to depend on you so much that I feel threatened when you go out."

"There's no need. Jack's fine if I want a good laugh, but that's all. Depend on me all you like. I'm not going anywhere."

He considered her, smiling. "It's incredible. In the short time you've been with us you've transformed my home and my relationship with my son, and yet I still know almost nothing about you."

"There's nothing to know," she said. "What you see is what you get."

"No, you're full of mysteries. You told me you'd been in love nine years ago, and it would be the last time. What happened, Melanie? How can you be so sure?"

"Did I say that? I don't remember."

"I think you do. Why are you trying to put me off?"

She shrugged, not meeting his eyes. "Girls of sixteen are always being disillusioned with love."

"Yes, but they grow out of it. With you it's lasted nine years, and you're still disillusioned. It must have been something terrible."

Melanie threw a crumb of fish to a hopeful bird. She was refusing to look at Giles as he inched nearer to the secret that would destroy her in his eyes. "I don't want to talk about it," she said.

"Then it *was* something terrible?"

"I said I don't want to talk about it," she repeated sharply. Alarm filled her. She rose abruptly and began to walk away. Giles hailed the waiter, stuffed some money into his hands and chased after her.

"Melanie—Melanie, I'm sorry." He caught up with her in the shadow of the trees and pulled her around to face him. She could feel the hair of his chest rasping slightly against her arm, and suddenly the modest one-piece felt as skimpy as a bikini.

"Don't ever pry into my private affairs, Giles."

"I didn't mean to intrude. It's just important to me to know about you."

"It doesn't need to be—"

"But it is," he said, holding her more insistently. "You know why, don't you?"

Yes, she knew why, because the clamor in her blood was telling her. The pounding was blotting out rational thought, sending her into a spin in which caution was almost forgotten. She struggled to cling onto her common sense, but it was hard when he was so close.

"You know what's happening to us, don't you?" he persisted. "You know I've wanted to kiss you all day. Right now I'd like to take you back to the chalet and kiss you all over, and then—"

"But you can't!" she cried. "I won't let you. I *mustn't.*"

She wrenched herself out of his hold and ran as hard as she could. She had a glimpse of his face, astonished and haggard, before she fled, seeking to put as much distance between them as possible.

She ran inland until she was breathless, then turned and made her way back to the shore. There was no longer any sign of Giles, but he might return at any moment. If only she could get out alone onto the lake, she thought, she could come to terms with what was happening to her. There was one small yacht left at the boat center, but the man was reluctant to hire it to her.

"It will soon be dark, *signorina,*" he protested.

"I only want it for a little while," she said, and he shrugged and gave way.

She pulled out into deep water. Here at least there was peace, and a chance to sort out her turbulent emotions.

On the face of it her situation looked so simple. To attach Giles to her would be the surest way of staying with David. A more calculating woman would have seized that option, especially after the fright she'd had. But Melanie had made her plans in the days when Giles had been a monster and her emotions had slept. Now he was no monster but a troubled, vulnerable and disturbingly attractive man, who was beginning to turn to her. And she was full of confusion.

She stared into the water, seeming to see pictures dancing in its surface—herself, Giles and David, together for always. It was an enchanted vision. Then the picture changed, and there was only Giles and herself. David was still there in their lives, her love for him an everlasting thread in her love—her *feelings* for Giles, she amended hastily. But for the moment she was thinking only of the man who was inching his way into her heart. He seemed to smile at her from the water, and she smiled back.

The boat lurched suddenly, almost throwing her overboard. She grabbed hold of the side and fought to get the little vessel under control again. It was hard, because a stiff wind had blown up and the boat was bobbing wildly. While she'd been lost in her daydream the weather had changed for the worse, and a storm was brewing. She looked around her. She was almost out of sight of land in all directions, and it was growing darker by the minute, but by straining her eyes she could just make out the shore from which she'd come.

It took all her skill to turn the boat and head back. It was starting to rain and the light was fading as the sky grew overcast. She'd heard that storms could whip up in minutes in this part of the world, but she could hardly believe the speed with which everything had changed.

Waves lashed the boat, tossing her this way and that, while rain blinded her and the darkness gathered.

As she neared the shore she could see Giles standing there anxiously watching for her. He half pulled her out of the boat and into his arms. "I saw you take the boat out," he said. "When the weather changed I went crazy thinking of you out there, all alone. *Melanie—*"

At any other time she would have melted blissfully into his embrace, but now a new terror had entered her mind. She pulled herself free and ran to an official from the warden's office, who was staring out over the water. "The *Margarita,*" she cried. "Is there any news of her?"

He shrugged. "We've heard nothing, but this weather won't trouble her."

"But it's a storm—"

"A very small storm, *signora*. In a tiny boat like yours, very big. But to the *Margarita*—no problem."

"He's right," Giles said, coming up beside her. "I'm not too happy about David being out in this, in case he's scared. But I don't think there's any danger."

Reluctantly she let herself be led away to the chalet. Her mind was fixed on David, perhaps frightened as the boat was tossed about, but she tried to be sensible and tell herself that she was making too much of it.

When she'd showered and dried herself off she emerged to find Giles waiting for her with a hot drink that he'd made himself. "Drink this and try not to worry," he said. "That man was right. This isn't as big a storm for the *Margarita* as it was for you in the small boat."

At that moment there came a flash of lightning, soon followed by a crack of thunder. "Oh, God, listen to that!" she said wildly. "You shouldn't have let him go. How could you do it?"

"I didn't know this was going to happen."

"How could you let him go off with strangers?" She knew she was being irrational but the words poured out despite herself. "Total strangers and you let them take your son—"

"They're not quite total strangers are they?" he retorted grimly. "You and Jack seem friendly enough."

"What's that got to do with anything?" she cried. They were deafened by another crack of thunder. As it roared and grumbled overhead they stared at each other, Melanie distraught, Giles with a strange look, as though the violence of her emotion had taken him aback. "Listen to that," she said. "What must it be like out on the lake? Oh, God! David! *David.*"

She turned and ran out of the chalet. Giles made as if to go after her, but the ringing of the phone stopped him. Melanie heard nothing. She was lost in a world where there was only agonizing fear for her little son. Rain was coming down in sheets now, but she battled her way through it to race down to the water's edge. *"David,"* she screamed. *"David."*

She didn't know how long she stood there, but it seemed to be for ages, while the rain lashed her and the wind whipped her hair across her face. She strained to see into the darkness, but all she could see was the turbulent water.

There was a hand on her shoulder and she whirled around. "Giles, we've got to do something," she begged.

"Melanie, listen—"

"We must call out the rescue service. Anything could have happened to him. You should never have let him go."

"Melanie!" He gave her a little shake.

"How can you just stand there?" she cried. "Your son might be drowning—"

"But he isn't. Listen to me. I've just had a phone call from the Fraynes. It's all right. When the weather started to look bad they put into shore. They're in a hotel at the north end of the lake."

"What?" she stared at him. It was too big to take in all at once.

"David's perfectly safe. I've just spoken to him."

Melanie gave a gasp. Her whole body shook with the violence of her relief after anguish. "Thank God!" she whispered. "Oh, thank God!"

Giles stared at her, astounded. He knew that her love for David went far beyond the ordinary, but even so, the intensity of her emotion startled him. He took hold of her gently, but the feel of her quivering body was too much for him. "Come on," he said, pulling her against him. "It's all right, he's safe."

"I can't help it," she wept. "It's just that—"

"I know," he murmured. "I know."

"You don't know. How can you be so calm?"

"Because he's not in any danger. It's over now." He tightened his arms about her, stroking her hair. "Let's go inside before you catch cold."

He kept one arm firmly about her until they were in the chalet. Then he pushed her down onto the sofa. She was shivering, from shock more than cold, so he poured her a brandy and forced it into her hands. "What did David say?" she asked. "Oh, I wish I could have talked to him."

"You can. I've got the number of the hotel." He dialed, and in a few moments was talking to David. "Melanie wants a word with you," he said, and passed the phone over.

"Darling, are you all right?" she demanded tensely.

"'Course I am," said her son's eager voice. "It's smashing here. There's a pirate exhibition and—"

She hardly heard the rest in the joy of hearing his voice, robust and happy. When Giles gently took the phone from her she gave a shaky laugh. "All he could talk about was the pirate exhibition," she said.

"That's children for you."

"Yes—yes, it is...." Her control was slipping away. Next moment she put her face in her hands and sobbed. Giles didn't waste words, but drew her into his arms and soothed her. "That's what I feel like doing," he said wryly.

"We might have lost him," she cried. She thought of the eight weary years without her child, and the little time she'd had him back, and fresh sobs shook her. "Eight years—eight years—"

"What was that?" He bent his head to catch her muffled words.

"I said—he's only eight years old—" she said quickly.

"I know. And I'd only just begun to know him—to lose him now—but we didn't lose him. Hold onto that."

She made a massive effort to control herself, and lifted her head. Giles looked down at her. With her hair tumbling about and the ravages of emotion on her face, she looked young and vulnerable, and suddenly he did what he'd been wanting to do for days. He tightened his arms and kissed her.

"Giles—" she whispered.

"Don't say anything," he begged. "We've both known that this was bound to happen."

He spoke with his lips against hers, and drew her against him again. Melanie felt her strength slip away from her. She couldn't resist. She could only yield to what, as Giles had said, was inevitable. She'd seen his eyes on her and lived this kiss in her imagination. Now it was here, a hundred times sweeter than her fevered longing had promised.

Her conscience told her that she should protest, that while she was deceiving him it was wrong to melt in his arms, but she couldn't help herself. The sweet urgency of his passion overwhelmed her. At this moment there was nothing she wanted so much as to be here, with this man who'd brought her heart to life, giving and taking.

He kissed her gently, like a man who'd promised himself this for a long time and wasn't going to spoil it by hurrying. The slow, purposeful movement of his lips over hers gave her time to savor the heart-stopping sensation of beauty. He wanted her as much as she wanted him. That alone gave her an astonished delight that her lonely life had never offered before.

"Giles—" she murmured.

"Hush, darling. Don't stop me. I've wanted to kiss you for so long—didn't you know?"

"Yes—yes—"

"I didn't imagine it, did I? It's been there between us—" The last word was muffled as he covered her mouth again.

She couldn't think any more about whether she had any right to do this. She could only yield helplessly to what she urgently desired. His mouth on hers felt right, as though this had been intended from the beginning of time. Sweetness and warmth flooded her body, almost shocking her with its intensity. It was so long since any man had held her in his arms, so long since she'd felt desire, and then it had betrayed her. She was afraid of passion, but fear fell back before the feelings sweeping her now. Giles's mouth was firm yet gentle on hers, tempting her with sweet delights that she couldn't resist.

She gave a long, tremulous sigh that made him draw back and look at her. "Melanie," he whispered. "My sweet Melanie—kiss me—*kiss me*—"

He pressed her back against the cushions, covering her face with kisses. At the touch of his lips something flowered within her. Since the moment, weeks ago, when she'd come back to life, she'd known, deep in her heart, that this joy was waiting for her. She'd fled from it, but there had been no escape. This man, once her enemy, was the one her heart longed for, the one who could make her body sing with delight, and now she no longer wanted to escape. She wanted to open heart and mind and body to him, willing to be whatever he desired, if only she could be his.

She offered him her mouth, parting her lips to invite him and holding him tight in a gesture of affirmation and possession. He understood and claimed her mouth, exploring the silky skin inside with small flickering movements of his tongue that sent sparks of pleasure through her.

She'd forgotten what it was like to be kissed with tenderness and joy. Or rather, she had never known. The selfish fumblings that had passed for love with Oliver had been all she knew of relations between men and women, and they'd left her with no taste for any more. Now she was learning that a man could rein back his desire, subtly seeking her response, waiting until she was ready for more. She was learning that her own desire could come rushing up, reveling in the freedom that he gave her by his restraint. Released from the atmosphere of petulant impatience that had blighted her only other experience, she could relax and let her heart and soul revel in delight.

Giles drew back to look down at where she lay against her cushions. His eyes were shining. "I've been such a fool," he murmured. "I was jealous of Jack Frayne—tell me I didn't need to be."

"You know you didn't," she told him, laughing with sheer pleasure at the discovery that he could be jealous.

"I know—at least, I think I do. But I want to hear you say it."

"You have nothing to be jealous of," she said fervently. "Nothing."

"Even though he's an Adonis?" Giles queried. Melanie shook her head. "With charm that no woman can resist?" he persisted.

"You were right," she whispered. "You really are a fool." She pulled his head down toward her, and this time the kiss was hers. She moved her lips sensuously over his, luxuriating in the feel of him against her, the firmness and mobility of his mouth, the marvelous smell of sun and wind and maleness.

With gentle hands he opened the buttons of her shirt and pulled the edges apart to reveal her breasts. The touch of his fingers was light, but even so it sent forks of fire through her, making her gasp and arch herself in eager expectation. He touched her softly, teasing her nipples to peaks of desire before bending his head to take one between his lips. Melanie moaned with pleasure and threaded her fingers through his dark hair, yielding herself utterly to the rapturous sensation. Tremors of pleasure went through her at the skillful movements of his tongue. Inside her a miracle was happening, banishing the sadness of years, reviving her with the promise of life.

And then he spoiled it.

"Melanie," he murmured, "my sweet, perfect Melanie..."

On the word "perfect" a small cloud appeared in her mind. She tried to ignore it but it grew until it loomed darkly over her. She knew how far from perfect she was, how she had deceived him and was forced to go on deceiving him. She would gladly have told him the truth, but she didn't dare. And now her conscience seized on that terrifying word, "perfect," worrying it back and forth, while passion died in her, to be replaced by fear.

He sensed her inner withdrawing and raised his head. His breath was coming raggedly, but he had himself under control. "What is it?" he asked huskily. "What's wrong?"

"Nothing," she stammered, feeling the precious moment slip away.

"Yes, something's wrong. I felt you go away from me." He pulled back from her quickly, as though he felt safer with a distance between them. Melanie did up her buttons. She was filled with despair at what had happened. It was her own fault, and there was nothing she could do about it.

"What is it, Melanie?" Giles asked quietly. "Don't try to tell me it's nothing. Is it David? Are you still worrying about him?"

"Yes—no—it's not David," she said wildly. "I know I'm being silly but—"

"No," he said at once. "I don't think you're being silly. I'm going too fast for you, aren't I? It's just that I—that what you've become to me—no, let that wait. I know something happened in the past that hurt you badly. I don't know what it was, because you don't trust me enough to tell me yet, but I hope one day you will. In the meantime, the last thing I want to do is hurt you again. So we'll just leave it there for the moment."

She could have wept at his understanding. When she looked at his face all desire had been wiped from it, leaving only warmth and kindness. "I'll wait until you're ready," he said. "But darling, don't let it be too long."

She answered him, not in words, but in a soft kiss that gave him reassurance. They stayed like that, locked in each other's arms, occasionally dozing, until the dawn broke, and through the window they could see the *Margarita's* sails in the distance. He seized her hand and they ran out together to see David, waving at them in the prow. In no time at all the boat was in and he was running ashore to hurl himself into their outstretched arms, which closed around him, so that the three of them became one.

Seven

Melanie parked the car that Giles now kept for her use, and went around the house to enter through the French doors. Her arms were laden with parcels, for in the week they'd been home she'd already started equipping David for his next term at school. He was a happier child now, more at ease with his father, but still with a caution that made him cling to Melanie, as though fearful that everything might be snatched away again.

There'd been a strange car parked outside the house, so she guessed he had a visitor and probably wouldn't want to be disturbed. As she went into the hall she was arrested by the sound of Giles's angry voice coming from his office. "I wish you'd try to realize the effect this has on David," he was saying. "I've told you before how upset it's all made him."

A woman answered, sounding weary and petulant.

"And I've told you why I felt a clean break would be best for everyone."

Melanie froze. Even after eight years, she remembered that voice, with its chilly self-satisfaction. Shivers of horror went through her as she realized that she was only a few feet away from Zena, the one person who could identify her and bring her whole world tumbling down.

"The best for you, you mean," Giles said bitterly. "Let's be honest. 'Loverboy' didn't want the inconvenience of a child, did he? I'll bet he made you promise to ditch David before he married you."

"By 'loverboy' I suppose you mean Antony. No, he didn't want David. Why should he? Why should *I?* You were the one who wanted a child, not me."

"You were David's mother for eight years. It broke his heart when you left. You could at least have the decency to see him sometimes, to make it easier on him. I want you to wait and meet Melanie—"

"Is that really necessary?"

"You're a hard-hearted woman Zena, but even you'll be touched at what Melanie can tell you—how he's been recently—how he misses you."

"All right, if I must."

Holding her breath, Melanie began to creep backward, her eyes still fixed on the open door of Giles's office. As she moved she prayed that nobody would come out and see her. Her prayers were answered. She reached the French doors, then turned and ran back to the garage. She managed to get the car out quietly, then drove away as fast as she dared.

But she knew that she'd obtained only a temporary reprieve. She didn't dare go back to the house while there was a chance that Zena was there. And that meant a long time.

Someday soon she would tell Giles the truth. But not yet, and not like this. Heaven knows what the revelation would do to the fragile web of love and trust that was growing between them, though if he learned in the right way, she might survive it. But nothing could be worse than to have Zena recognize her and spew out the truth, filtered through her own spiteful mind.

It was three hours before Melanie returned home, and then she checked carefully to make sure Zena's car had gone. It had, but there was another one in its place. It had evidently just drawn up, and a slim, middle-aged woman was getting out. Giles appeared at the door, scowling as he saw the other woman. "Good evening, Mrs. Braddock," he said coolly.

"I've come to see David," she announced in an equally frosty voice.

Giles's face lightened as he saw Melanie, and she hurried forward. "I'm afraid David isn't here just now," he said. "He's staying overnight with a school friend." He ushered them all through the front door. "This is Melanie Haynes, who looks after him for me."

Mrs. Braddock eyed Melanie up and down, taking in her youth and beauty, and appearing to be offended by them. She shook the hand Melanie held out but didn't favor her with a greeting. "I called last week," she said in a precise voice that tinkled disagreeably on Melanie's ear. "He wasn't here, either. None of you were." She made it sound a cause for suspicion.

"We were on holiday," Melanie said, speaking as pleasantly as she could manage. "We went sailing on the Italian lakes. David had the time of his life."

"Indeed? And how did he feel about his mother's remarriage?"

Giles drew in his breath and his eyes met Melanie's, each of them wondering how Mrs. Braddock had acquired that information and what use she would make of it.

"He didn't seem particularly upset when I told him," Giles said evenly. "He knows that the break between us is final, and he's formed a bond with Miss Haynes."

"Hmm. When you say he didn't seem upset, you mean he didn't show any reaction. That can be a dangerous sign in a disturbed child—"

"No, that is not what I meant," Giles said, pale with anger. "David took it in his stride. In fact he's going to stay with Zena and her new husband next week. I assure you, he's adjusting very well to having two homes."

"That remains to be seen. I shall continue to monitor the situation, but I must tell you that I'm not satisfied."

They watched her go, and neither spoke until she was out of sight. Then Giles said, "That woman frightens me."

"And me," Melanie said. "She's made up her mind in advance."

"What took you so long? I had Zena here and I made her wait to talk to you, but you're hours late."

"I'm sorry. I went for a drive—it's such a lovely car—and got a bit lost."

Another lie, she thought, feeling the weight of them all like a crushing burden. *I'll tell him soon. I must.*

Aloud, she said, "Will she really have him to visit next week?"

"Luckily, yes. But I don't know what effect it will have on him, and with Mrs. Braddock 'monitoring the situation'—oh, hell, kiss me, Melanie." He pulled her into his arms without waiting for an answer, and she embraced him back joyfully. "I kept longing for you to come home," he murmured between kisses. "I cling to you just like David does. However do you put up with the two of us?"

She didn't answer him in words. She wouldn't have known what words to use. The trust in his voice hurt her conscience. So she told him of her love silently, with the urgent movements of her lips and the tenderness of her caresses, and wondered if the day would ever come when she could be completely open with him.

Both Giles and Melanie had expected David to be delighted at the prospective visit to Zena and her new husband, but his reaction was more mixed. One moment he seemed to look forward to going, the next he was clinging to Melanie, making her promise that she would still be there when he returned.

"Can I take your picture with me?" he asked her.

"I don't have one, darling."

"Daddy's got a camera. We could take one."

"There isn't time."

"Yes, there is—"

She felt caught on the prongs of a fork. It was wonderful to know that David wanted to keep her image by him, but she didn't dare let him have a picture. Somehow she managed to talk him out of it, but how long could she keep this up, she wondered? It was clear that in David's mind she was becoming an alternative mother, but just how seriously he took this was something she didn't discover until the morning of his departure.

She was in David's room, doing some last-minute packing, when she pulled open a drawer, and what she found there made her stare.

"What is it?" Giles asked, coming in.

"These things," she said in a dazed voice, lifting some of the contents of the drawer. "That's my pendant, and these are my gloves. I've been wondering where they were."

Giles groaned. "Oh, my God!" he exclaimed in despair. "He's stealing again. I thought he was over that. David."

"No, Giles, wait—"

"It's got to be dealt with, Melanie."

"Don't frighten him. I don't think this is quite what it seems."

"Stealing is stealing. There's no excuse for it." David appeared in the doorway. "Did you take these?" Giles demanded. David nodded silently.

"Why, darling?" Melanie asked quickly. "Don't be afraid. We're not angry. We just want to understand."

Tears had sprung into the child's eyes. "I wanted something of yours," he whispered. "You wouldn't let me take a picture, so I took something else."

"But you should have asked first," Giles said, speaking gently, to Melanie's relief. "Taking someone else's things without asking is wrong."

David sniffed. "But you do it."

Giles stared. "When have you ever known me to steal things?"

"Melanie's scarf," David said. "The one she lost in Italy. You said it had gone into the water, but you've had it all the time."

Giles opened his mouth and closed it again. Melanie looked at him. "Have you got my scarf?"

"Well—yes—I found it—"

"But you told me you hadn't," she reminded him. Seeing him speechless, she took pity on him. "Why don't you go downstairs? I'll be down in a minute."

Before he could leave, David asked quickly, "Am I bad, Daddy?"

Giles grinned and leaned down to his son like a conspirator. "We're both bad," he said ruefully.

When they were alone Melanie said to David, "You can keep one of these if you like. Which one?"

"The gloves," David said at once. "Because they smell like you. That's why Daddy wanted the scarf, too. I saw him put it against his face."

"Did you, darling?" It was hard to speak through the wild and whirling joy that possessed her.

"Why didn't he tell you?"

"Perhaps he didn't know how to. Sometimes people have feelings—that confuse them—and that are just too hard to talk about."

As she said the words, she wondered whose feelings she really meant, Giles's or her own. She was about to say more when she saw that David was nodding in perfect comprehension. Of course, she thought. Most of *his* feelings were hard to talk about.

"Won't you come with us?" Giles asked when he was ready to depart with David. "I thought if you could talk to Zena—"

"Giles, that's the worst idea you ever had," Melanie said quickly. "Keep Zena and me in separate compartments. My relationship with David has nothing to do with her."

He thought briefly. "You're right," he said. "I won't be long."

He met her eyes, and the thought of the scarf lay between them. But this wasn't the time. When he returned they would have much to say to each other. Melanie's heart beat faster as she thought of what some of those things might be.

She kissed David goodbye and watched the car vanish down the drive. Mrs. Wade was putting her apron away. "I've just finished," she said. "Is it all right if I go a bit early? I promised Sylvia we'd go to that waxwork exhibition. She's set her heart on seeing the Chamber of Horrors."

Melanie laughed. "Go on. I'll see you on Monday."

When she was alone she became thoughtful. Soon Giles would return and they would say—what? He'd kept her scarf and buried his face in it. Such a gesture meant more than passion. From a man like Giles that was practically a declaration of love, and her own heart surged to meet it, with joy.

But did she dare? The risks were so enormous, and yet...

She went upstairs and began to tidy her room, moving mechanically while her mind turned this way and that. She'd been foolish to imagine that the situation could remain static. If Giles hadn't turned to her he would have turned to some other woman, and her own position would have been under threat. Common sense dictated that she should seize her chance and marry him if possible.

But she didn't want to use common sense with Giles. She wanted there to be only love, freely given. She wanted passion and laughter and trust. And there lay the problem. If she let this go any further she would have to tell him the truth, and the minute she did that his trust would be shattered.

The risk was too great. When he returned in a few minutes she must put him off with a cool speech about being sensible. She began to order the words, ignoring the ache in her heart. She'd come too far to risk everything now.

She was so absorbed with her thoughts that she didn't hear the return of Giles's car, or his footsteps on the stairs. He came running to find her and stopped in the doorway to her room. She glanced up quickly. "Giles, I've been thinking and—"

But at the expression on his face all words died. She could only look at him, and love.

"Melanie," he said awkwardly. "About your scarf— I know it must seem odd but—*Melanie.*"

The next moment she was in his arms. All her hard-won common sense fell away as she yielded herself blissfully to the kiss she'd longed for. It felt good to be held so vigorously by this strong yet vulnerable man.

Then she felt him stiffen and push her away so that he could look into her face. His own face was riven with anxiety, and suddenly she understood. "It's all right, my love," she whispered. "This time it's different. Oh, Giles, I can't stay away from you."

"Why should you want to?"

"Because—because of a thousand reasons."

"There isn't one good reason that can come between us now," he said in an unsteady voice. "I wish you wouldn't keep things from me. I wish you trusted me enough to share your mystery. But I'm not afraid of it now. It can't change anything between us."

He tightened his arms again before she could answer, and in the sweet, ecstatic feel of his lips on hers, everything was lost but the moment. He was right, she thought, through the whirling of her senses. Nothing could change this. Nothing mattered but this.

She felt him lift her high against his chest, and she put her arms around his neck. A few strides took them to his bedroom. She kicked the door closed behind them, her lips on his, her whole attention given to loving him. Her time had come, and she was going to allow herself to savor it to the fullest.

He laid her down on the bed, raining kisses over her face, her neck. She gasped his name, in a fever of excitement as she felt his desire for her rising, and her own surging to meet it. This time it was she who pulled open the buttons of her own shirt, eager to feel the skilful touch of his hands and lips on her skin. Every inch of her was burning for him, and when she felt him lay his mouth against one peaked nipple she moaned helplessly.

His tongue began a lazy circling motion that almost sent her out of her mind. In the same instant she knew that this wasn't enough. She wanted him completely. He'd told her that he was a man who didn't believe in half measures, and now she knew that half measures wouldn't do for her, either. What was between them must be complete: complete passion, complete surrender and complete love.

She undid his buttons with determined, urgent fingers. He seemed astonished, but then surprise was replaced with delight and he began to throw off his clothes. Then all barriers had gone and there was just the two of them, naked, free to be themselves and give to each other.

For a moment the unfamiliarity of passion made her feel as awkward as an ignorant girl. But it passed. This man regarded her as precious. She could tell by the reverence in his face. He gazed on her for a long time as if he couldn't believe what he was seeing. Then he reached out to touch her gently. He let his hand drift down and along her contours, moving with slow wonder. He was like a man in a dream, half expecting to awaken at any second. It had never occurred to Melanie that her body had a beauty that could inspire awe. Oliver's selfish gropings had left her feeling demeaned, and no other man had been allowed near.

"I've dreamed of seeing you like this," he murmured against her mouth. "I'd begun to think it would never happen—that you didn't want me."

"I wanted you," she said huskily, "but the time wasn't right."

"And it's right now?"

"Everything's right now," she said fervently.

As though the words were a signal, he immediately deepened the kiss, sliding his tongue between her lips and starting a determined exploration of her mouth. His movements were slow but purposeful, and she relaxed, giving herself into the hands of a man whose every gesture proclaimed him a skilled lover. She could trust him, even though the tide of excitement that began to flow through her was more powerful than anything she'd ever known. As long as his strong arms held her with such tenderness and his mouth teased and incited her so cleverly, she knew she was safe.

As her confidence grew, she began to tease him back, offering herself to his kisses and caresses, and taking pleasure in the shape and feel of his body. The hot insistence of male desire enthralled her and made her confident in her own womanhood. With every passionate caress he was telling her she was special, she was the woman who could take him to the heights, and with all her soul she longed to be that woman.

She wanted everything that was happening, wanted the steel circle of his arms that protected her as though he knew how vulnerable she felt. She wanted the feeling of being caught up in something too strong for her. For years she'd had to impose an iron control on herself, but now she could toss that control aside and revel in the freedom of something she was powerless to resist. The tense, restrained woman she'd been at their first meeting had discovered the joys of recklessness. And it was Giles who'd made her a gift of this boundless liberty.

She began to move easily in his arms, offering her body to his love, making little incoherent sounds that were sometimes his name and sometimes gasps of pleasure and surprise. Everything about Giles's lovemaking was a revelation of what love could be. She learned that passion could be generous as well as ardent, tender and patient at the very moment of fiercest urgency. He entered her slowly, easily, giving her time to come to terms with him. And always his smile was there, full of delight and a kind of wonder that was like her own, as though he too had made a miraculous discovery. "My love," he whispered. "Melanie, my love..."

The words released the last of her inhibitions. With a cry of gladness she seized him against her, telling him without words how much she wanted him. He understood and the slow, powerful thrusts became deeper, more intense, as though with every one he was saying that she was his, and his alone. She picked up the message, received it gladly, and answered it with eager movements of her hips. All problems vanished. Only this existed, timeless, joyful, magic. She reached out longing hands for what was offered, and at the same instant the world became white-hot, whirling and spinning, catching her up in the everlasting motion, until it slowed and she was herself again.

He held her tightly until she grew calmer. She looked up at him with shining eyes and touched his face, exhausted and utterly happy.

Eight

Melanie awoke to find herself wrapped in Giles's arms. A faint light had crept into the room and she disengaged herself gently and sat up to look at him. In the melee of last night, the sheet had slipped onto the floor, and now she was free to enjoy his naked magnificence to her heart's delight. He lay stretched out, one arm thrown over his head, the harsh lines of his face softened, his lean, hard body relaxed in sleep, his chest rising and falling.

She longed to reach out a hand and run it down the length of his body, over the narrow hips, whose driving power had brought her such shattering pleasure, and the long, muscular thighs. But she didn't want to risk awakening him, so she contented herself with feasting her eyes.

She was no longer the person she'd been a few hours earlier. In the magic of his arms that tense, unfulfilled

creature had slipped away forever, replaced by someone who felt truly a woman for the first time. Her mind
went back to the morning when she'd become aware of
the sights and sounds of the world. Now she'd discovered life itself, her heart open to joy, her body alive to
pleasure.

She knew that there was love in the world, not only
mother love, but love between a man and a woman. It
nourished and renewed, opened up vistas of light and
beauty and hope for the future, and she wondered how
she'd survived so long without it.

She slipped quietly out of bed and went to the window, drawing back the curtain a few inches. Already the
small birds were beginning the dawn chorus. She
thought of that other dawn when she'd found him in the
garden and begun to understand him for the first time.
For her, dawn had truly come, a bright, glorious dawn,
full of promise.

From behind her she heard a voice, drowsy with sa-
tiation and content. "Come back here."

She sauntered over to the bed, moving with teasing
slowness, conscious of his eyes caressing her, and stood
there regarding him. With a sudden growl he seized her
and pulled her down. "I said come here." Laughing,
she sprawled on top of him and struggled, not too seriously, until he had her imprisoned in the circle of his
arms. "Now try and get away," he said.

She struggled again, relishing the sensation of her
skin moving against his. He held her easily, smiling into
her eyes. "Give up?"

"Mmm," she said blissfully, snuggling against him.
"Anytime you like."

He said no more. The playful wrestling match had
aroused them both and he began kissing her again ur-

gently, while his hands roved over her naked body, setting off exquisite tremors. Last night they'd started to get acquainted as lovers. There was still much to learn in the years ahead, but already they were no longer strangers. Her instincts were alive to him. Deep in her flesh she knew the little moves that pleased him, knew them on an unconscious level that made her body move in tune to his as though the two of them were one.

She ran her hands over his chest and down to his hips as easily as a practised seducer would have done. This, too, was one of the pleasures of passion that was being revealed to her, the knowledge that she could tease and incite her lover, caressing him where he found it hard to resist. The tremors that shook him at her touch gave her a special delight. He wanted her. He couldn't help responding to her, and she gloried in her power.

"My love..." she murmured. "My lover...my love..." Such sweet words, which had never passed her lips before.

The feel of his lips about one peaked nipple made her gasp with delight. He teased it gently, while electric forks sparked through her, making her whole body vibrate with excitement. "Yes..." she murmured ecstatically.

"There's so much we have to discover together," he whispered. "Come with me...."

"Anywhere..." She ran her hands through his springy dark hair. Every part of him felt good to her. She arched against him, giving herself up utterly to what was happening. She'd been dead to sensation for so long that it was almost shocking to discover how quickly she could be aroused. Their first loving had transformed her into the woman nature had always meant her to be, deeply sensual, eager to explore. She wanted to learn everything, and experience everything but only with this man.

Giles's instincts understood the change. The woman in his arms was no longer a cautious learner. He looked at her flushed face and a sigh of delight broke from him. She parted her legs and pulled him over her, willing him on to enter her and crying aloud when he did so. She drove her hips against him, reveling in the sense of oneness, and he loved her with more vigor than he'd dared use before, knowing that now she was ready. When their moment came she wrapped her legs around him possessively as the pleasure mounted to new heights. At the very last second she had a tantalizing glimpse of more peaks in the distance, still to be scaled. But not today. She was coming down to reality, finding herself where she wanted to be, in the arms of the man she loved.

He looked at her adoringly. "Well?" he asked, with a hint of humor.

Melanie smiled impishly. "Let's get some breakfast. I'm famished."

He gave a crack of laughter and tightened his arms until she gasped for breath, and they lay chuckling like children enjoying an idiotic joke.

With the house to themselves they were free to wander around dressed or undressed as they pleased. Melanie started to head for the kitchen to prepare a snack, wearing only a short nightgown and slippers. They almost had their first quarrel over the slippers, because she didn't want to bother and he insisted that the tiles would give her cold feet. The argument ended in him fetching the slippers from her room, tossing her onto the bed and inserting her feet in them by sheer strength. Then he found that she looked so irresistible, lying there with her hair tousled, that he got back into bed with her, and breakfast was late.

He came downstairs, collected a load of mail from the mat and deposited it, unopened, in his office, closing the door on it. After that he followed her into the kitchen and sat munching the savories she made. In the middle of this, the telephone rang. "I guess we can't really shut out the world," Melanie said regretfully.

"Can't I? You watch me." Before her fascinated eyes he went out into the hall and switched on the answering machine.

"But suppose it's important?" she asked.

"Listen."

The answerphone had picked up the call and they could hear a voice saying urgently, "Giles, I need to contact you. Van Lyman is arriving in this country tomorrow. When you get this message call him on—"

"Van Lyman will just have to manage without me," Giles said, turning down the volume and putting his arms around her.

"They won't give up," Melanie prophesied. "They'll try your mobile phone."

He grinned. "I switched it off."

She stared. "You switched your mobile phone off?" she asked comically. "Do you realize you're out of contact with the world? Oh, no, there's always the fax machine."

"It's on automatic. It can spew paper out to its heart's content, but who says I have to read it?"

"You're mad," she said, and laughed.

"That's right. Gloriously mad, and I'm enjoying every moment of it." He put his arms around her. "Who wants to be sane?"

They spent the day as idiotically as possible. If they were hungry they ate cornflakes and anything else that didn't need much preparation. At other times they curled up on the sofa together, watching television shows that were the equivalent of wallpaper. She loved to make him laugh. He laughed like a man who'd only recently discovered how, and the sound filled her heart with tenderness.

"Let's see what's next," she said in the late afternoon as she lay back against him, turning the pages of the TV magazine. "'Guess My Hobby.' Another highly intellectual program."

He yawned and stretched. "It's all I can aspire to at the moment. My brains feel about the rough consistency of mushy peas."

She prodded him. "That's why you made such a mess of that last answer," she jeered.

"I did not," he said indignantly. "I had it right."

"Not according to Maxie—You Lovely People—Derwent."

"Maxie—You Lovely People—Derwent wears a glitter jacket," Giles said, as though that settled the matter.

"What's that got to do with it?"

"Well, what can you expect from a man in a glitter jacket?"

"He was still right about *The Ugly Duckling*," Melanie insisted.

Giles was outraged. "He didn't know the first thing about *The Ugly Duckling*, and neither do you."

"Bad loser!"

"I did not lose. May you be forgiven! *I did not lose*."

"Why must you argue about everything?"

"Because I know I'm right. Here, shift yourself, woman. Let's get the encyclopedia."

"Yes, let's get the *children*'s encyclopedia," she mocked.

Still squabbling happily, they found the right volume and looked up the fairy tales of Hans Andersen. There followed a short silence.

"OK, so I was wrong about that," Giles said casually. "But he didn't know anything about—*hey, get off*."

"You're ticklish," she caroled delightedly. "Yes, you are."

"Yes, I am, and if you don't stop you'll be sorry."

He imprisoned her hands firmly, looking into her laughing face in a passion of tenderness. Slowly his mouth moved toward hers. Silence fell again and continued for a long time. Eventually he raised his head and said unsteadily, "Are we going to make love, or have something to eat?"

"Eat," she said prosaically.

"You have no soul," he complained, following her into the kitchen.

"Not when my stomach's empty, no."

She made omelets, which they devoured before going up to bed and lying contentedly in each other's arms. "What was that noise?" he asked at last as they were getting drowsy.

"What noise? I didn't hear a noise."

"You made it. You sniggered. There. You've done it again. What's so funny?"

"You. Knowing about fairy tales. If there was one man in the world I would have expected to know nothing at all about fairy tales it was you. Except the ones written by the brothers *Grimm,*" she added cheekily.

"Very funny!"

"So come on, tell me. How do you come to be such an expert?"

"I used to listen to my mother reading them."

"That conjures up a delightful picture."

"Not really. She didn't read them to me, but to my sister, Alice. I used to stay outside the door and listen."

"How sad! But why didn't you go in?"

He shrugged. "I wasn't wanted. I was four years older than Alice and supposedly too old for fairy tales. Well, it wasn't the tales themselves, it was the fact that my mother read them to her. I'd look in sometimes and see her sitting on my sister's bed, with Alice in the crook of her arm, looking at the book together. Neither of them noticed me. To my eyes they seemed enclosed in a golden circle that admitted no outsiders."

"Outsiders! But you were her son."

"She was one of those women who could manage only one love at a time. Alice got it all." He shrugged. "I didn't mind."

"Oh, sure, you didn't mind! You didn't mind so much that you used to stand outside the door."

"Boys aren't supposed to mind," he said. "So I told myself I didn't. After a while I believed it."

But the instincts of love told her that he minded to this very day. Melanie clenched her hands, filled with protective anger for the hurt little boy he'd once been. "Didn't she ever read to you?" she asked.

"I asked her to once. She said she would, but then Alice called her and she never came back. I fell asleep waiting." He made a sudden impatient sound. "How did we get onto this? It was all a long time ago."

"Come here," she said, drawing his head down to hers. The kiss she gave him was full of tender comfort, seeking to reach back and ease a hurt that time couldn't erase. But she would erase it, she promised herself, in all the years to come.

They dozed in each other's arms, and when she awoke she found him lying propped on one elbow, adoring her. "You're so different from any other woman I've known," he whispered. "I'm still cautious about saying or doing the wrong thing." A faint self-mocking smile touched his mouth. "Is it too soon to tell you that I love you?"

She smiled back, her eyes shining in the semidarkness. "It's never too soon to tell me that, my love."

"Isn't it? If I'd said it in Italy, would you have been ready to hear it? I wonder. You were so strange out there, sort of jumpy. And I was falling more in love with you every day." He grinned. "I was ready to kill Jack Frayne when you said he was an Adonis with a lot of charm."

She silenced him by laying her lips tenderly on his. Then she drew back to look at him, reveling in her miracle that had come at last. "Tell me that you love me," he pleaded.

"I love you, Giles."

Her heart was beating fast as she came to the moment of decision. Surely now she could tell him the truth? Now, when their hearts and minds were open and they were close to each other. She could tell him anything and it would only unite them further. She took a deep breath....

"You know," he said softly, before she could speak, "I can't believe this is really happening to me. To be loved by you is—unbelievable."

"Why should it be unbelievable, my love?"

He hesitated, and when he finally spoke again it was awkwardly, as though he were voicing something too painful for words. "Because I can't see myself as—as a man who could inspire love. Nobody has ever loved me wholeheartedly before. Not my mother, not Zena—nobody until you. My parents divorced when I was younger than David. My mother insisted on custody of both Alice and me, but I soon came to realize that she only wanted me to spite my father. To him I was the heir to Haverill & Son, and that gave her a weapon. She made him beg and plead for access. It's not the same as being wanted for yourself.

"I tried to deny the truth to myself for years because it's hard to admit that your mother doesn't love you. But when I forced myself to look at the way she treated Alice and the way she treated me, I knew the truth.

"And when I was a man, there was Zena. She told me she was pregnant, but after the wedding I discovered it was all a lie. She knew she couldn't have children. But I fooled myself. I told myself she must love me to be so anxious to marry me, and all the time I knew in my heart that it was the Haverill money she wanted.

"That's why David's love has always been so important. He was the only one who wasn't using me to get something else." He gave a short laugh. "I suppose I became a bit paranoid about it. I began to wonder if I was some kind of a monster, that there was something wrong with me that everyone else could see and I couldn't." He stroked Melanie's face slowly, as if held by a kind of wonder. "But then you came along and kissed the monster and he turned into—not a prince, but a man like other men, with a heart to love.

"I've known from the start that you were sweet and honest, and good all through. My heart tells me that, and this time I know I'm not fooling myself. Tell me that it's true. Let me hear you say it."

But at first she couldn't speak. Tears blurred her eyes at the way this proud man had humbly and trustingly told her his most wounding secret. She hated the mother whose selfish indifference had left him wandering, desolate, in search of a love that should have been his by right. She hated even more the wife who'd snared him with the promise of happiness, only to abandon him when she'd got what she wanted. The two women who should have loved him had only left him convinced that he was unworthy of love.

But then, with horror, she realized that this was no time for her confession. If Giles knew everything, how would she ever convince him that she loved him for himself, as well as for David?

Then she saw his eyes on her, full of sudden anxiety, and she realized that the problem would have to wait. Now the only thing that mattered was to reassure him, to give him the special glory that belonged to a man who knew he was utterly loved for himself alone.

"You don't really need me to tell you that I love you," she said softly. "You know it whenever I look at you. It must shine from my eyes. Sometimes I've had to turn my face away for fear of what you'd read there. I've fought it so hard—"

"But why, my darling? Why fight it?"

"I can't tell you that just now. It just didn't seem— wise to fall in love with you, but I couldn't help myself. You're the man I have to love, no matter what."

"No matter what?" he echoed in wonder. "You make it sound as if some harm could come from our love."

"No harm can come from the kind of love I feel for you," she said gravely. "As long as you trust it. If you know that I love you, we're safe."

"Then we're safe," he said, searching her face, trying to read it. "What can hurt us?"

"Nothing," she said. "Nothing. *Nothing*."

In the early evening they rose from bed and helped each other to dress. "Nearly six o'clock," he said, looking at his watch. "Let's go and collect David."

"I'll stay here," she said quickly. "Then I can have something ready for him to eat as soon as he gets home."

"Perhaps you're right. Let's have a thrown-together meal for the three of us."

She laughed and put her arms around him. "My poor darling, I should think you need a proper meal. To think I've always told David to steer clear of junk foods. If he knew what we've had for the last two days I'd never get him to eat sensibly again."

He kissed her nose. "Make sure he never finds out. I won't be long."

When he'd gone Melanie wandered into the kitchen, dazed with the happiness that had come to her so unexpectedly. Only a short time ago the world had been a bleak, empty place, but now the son she loved and the man she loved were both hers.

After an hour she looked at the clock, surprised that they hadn't returned. After two hours she was beginning to feel the first pricklings of alarm, when the phone rang.

"Melanie—" His voice sounded ravaged.

"Giles, what is it? What's happened?"

"David's vanished. When I reached Zena's house it was empty. They'd gone out and dumped David with a neighbor until I got there. But he ran away. I've been driving around, searching for him, but I can't find him anywhere."

"Oh, my God!" Melanie clenched her free hand, thinking of the child so callously dismissed yet again.

"He may be trying to walk home," Giles said. "I'm going to go on searching around here, but I want you to take the other car and look near the house."

She tore out to the garage and was on the road in a few seconds. There was still some light, but although she drove for an hour there was no sign of David and her panic grew. At last she went home to see if Giles had returned. He hadn't, but there was a message on the answering machine. "I haven't found him," he said bleakly. "I'm on my way back."

He arrived ten minutes later, his face gray and ghastly. She held him in her arms for a long moment before saying, "We're going to have to call the police."

"Yes," he said heavily. But as he stretched out his hand the telephone rang. Melanie fixed her eyes on him as he answered and saw his start of joy. "It's the police," he said. "They've found him. They want us to go and collect him."

"Thank God."

But when they were in the car, she said, "There's something wrong, isn't there?"

"I don't know," he said distractedly. "There was an odd note in the policeman's voice that told me it's not going to be simple when we get there. He said David's all right—I don't know what it could be—I just don't know—"

At the police station they approached the desk and Giles said tensely to the sergeant on duty, "My name is Giles Haverill. You have my son here."

"Ah, yes, Mr. Haverill. Would you just go into the interview room through there?"

"I'd like to see my son at once."

"I realize that, but there's someone in there who needs to talk to you first."

Giles seemed on the verge of losing his temper, but Melanie laid a quiet, warning hand on his arm. "All right," he said, taking hold of her hand and gripping it hard in a way that reminded her of David.

As soon as they entered the interview room, Giles drew in his breath on a sharp note of horror. Sitting there, talking to a woman police officer, was Mrs. Braddock. "I imagine you know why I'm here, Mr. Haverill," she said, rising and facing him. "I wonder if you're willing to admit now that the care of this child is completely beyond you?"

"I'm not responsible for his mother's selfish carelessness," Giles said harshly. "I've spent the last few hours searching for my son and I'd like to see him now."

"Just one moment." Mrs. Braddock held up her hand with an infuriating air of complacency. "I'm a professional, Mr. Haverill, trained to know what's best for disturbed children. Any child is better for having two parents and a stable home. I've told you before that I believe David should be put into care and—"

"*No.*" Melanie had listened in silence while her terror mounted. Now it broke forth in a violent exclamation. "How dare you call David disturbed," she snapped. "He's unhappy, and I'm *damned* if I'm going to let you label him for your files."

Mrs. Braddock stared at her as recognition dawned. "Oh, yes, the baby-sitter."

"Call me what you like. I look after David a sight better than Zena Haverill ever did."

Mrs. Braddock gave a sniff. "That's hardly to the point. David needs a proper home and I intend to see that he has one. It's best if I take him right now—"

"Over my dead body," Melanie raged. The next words burst from her before she could think. *"You're not touching my son."*

Mrs. Braddock's eyebrows rose. *"Your* son?"

"He will be soon," Melanie said quickly. "Mr. Haverill and I are getting married."

It was a wild improvisation, one she would have hardly dared if she'd had time to think. When the words were out the world seemed to stop while she prayed that Giles would back her up. Mrs. Braddock turned a suspicious gaze onto him.

"Indeed? Strange that Mr. Haverill didn't tell me so himself."

"I would have done if you'd let me get a word in edgeways," Giles said in a voice that was almost steady. "Miss Haynes has been caring for David for some time now, and he likes her. We're getting married as soon as possible. She'll be the perfect mother for him, and we'll fit your requirements for a two-parent family."

But Mrs. Braddock was made of stern stuff. She hesitated a moment but came back to respond, "You can argue that in court. For tonight I still think it's best if David comes with me, and I can promise you that the police will implement my instructions."

The woman police officer with her nodded, and said, "It really might be best if—"

From somewhere in the depths of the building there came a commotion. Melanie looked up as she heard David's voice, followed by the sounds of protest and running feet. The next moment the door had burst open and David tore into the room, pursued by two policemen. Mrs. Braddock put out a restraining hand but he brushed past her to hurl himself into Melanie's arms. The next moment his arms were about her neck and he was sobbing violently into her shoulder. Melanie picked him up and sat down with him in her lap while he poured out his grief. Over his head Melanie saw the three police officers exchange significant glances.

She held him tight while he tried to explain in choked, jumbled words. "—wanted to find you—got lost—she doesn't want me—you won't leave, will you? Please—"

"No, darling, I won't leave you ever," Melanie said. "I'll always be with you."

"Promise—*promise*—"

"I promise," she said firmly. Then she got to her feet, still holding David, whose face was buried against her neck. She ignored Mrs. Braddock and addressed the police. "I'm taking David out to the car. If any of you want to tear him away from me, you'd better try now."

It was a massive gamble but she'd judged perfectly. The three police officers stepped back to let her pass. One of them put a hand out to restrain Mrs. Braddock. Another opened the door for her. She walked out with her head high and her son in her arms.

Nine

There was no chance to talk on the way home. Giles drove and Melanie sat in the back seat with David on her lap. He was still distraught after his experiences, clinging to her and weeping. She tightened her arms around him and brushed her lips against his hair, seeking to comfort and reassure him.

Once home she carried him inside, but even here he was unwilling to relinquish his hold. So Melanie sat with him on her lap while he poured out the story. Between his choking sobs they gradually pieced together the tale of how Zena and her husband had been impatient to go out for the evening and had grown tired of waiting for Giles to arrive. At last the husband had snapped, "Dump the brat next door. They like kids, I don't." And Zena had made no protest.

"She doesn't want me—" David sobbed, "—because I'm bad."

"You're not bad," Melanie said desperately.

"I am, I am. That's why my other Mommy didn't want me—I'm bad, I'm bad."

"No." Melanie spoke with a fierceness that neither of them had ever heard in her before. Giles stared, and David's attention was distracted from his own grief. "You're not bad," she continued to say in the same fierce tone. "You're never to speak of yourself that way. You're a wonderful boy and we're both so proud of you."

"Are you going to be my Mommy now?" David asked simply.

"If you'll let me."

"And you won't leave me?"

"I won't leave you, ever. Neither will Daddy."

To the wonder of both of them, this reassurance acted like a spell on David. He rested his head against Melanie's shoulder and his eyes closed. But he wasn't asleep, because when she moved his arms tightened about her.

"I think you should go to bed," she said quietly.

Giles came up with her, and together they undressed David and put him between the sheets. Crying had exhausted him and he nodded off almost at once, his hand tucked into Melanie's. She waited until he was deeply asleep before gently freeing herself and creeping out of the room.

"He should sleep for a long time now," she said to Giles.

Giles took her hand. "Melanie," he said in a moved voice, "I don't know how to thank you—for everything. If it hadn't been for you—there aren't words—"

"We don't need words."

He took her face between his hands. "Did you mean what you said, about marrying me?"

"Of course I meant it—if it's what you want."

"It's what I want, but I have to know why. Is it just for David or—?" He couldn't go on.

"Not just for David," she promised him.

"Are you sure? I know there's always been some kind of special bond between you. I don't understand it, but I know it's there."

"Yes, it's there. But so is the bond between you and me. I love you, Giles. David will grow up and leave home, but I'll love you forever."

His eyes glowed with some emotion too deep for words. In another moment he would have kissed her, but suddenly, from upstairs they heard a scream.

"David!" Melanie said quickly. She ran up the stairs two at a time and threw open the door of David's room. He was sitting up in bed crying wildly, tears pouring down his face. "You went away," he sobbed. "I woke up and you weren't here."

"I was just downstairs," she said, enfolding him in her arms in a passion of tenderness. "I didn't really go away, and I never will. I promise."

"We're not going to let her go," Giles said. "We're going to keep her with us forever."

To Melanie's delight he took one of David's hands. She took the other, making the three of them a perfect circle. This was how it would always be in future, she thought. David snuggled down, still holding both of them as though this gave him the security he desperately needed. "Stay with me," he said.

Inspiration came to her. What she was about to do had been slowly developing in her mind for some time, waiting for the right moment. Now she knew the moment had come. "Shall I tell you a special story?" she asked, and he nodded.

"Very well. Once upon a time there was a witch called Seraphina."

"Was she very wicked?" David asked.

"No, she was a good witch. She practised only white magic, and looked after people whenever she could. She lived in a faraway country called the Land of Heart's Joy."

Melanie's voice grew soft. "Seraphina had a baby boy that she loved very much. Every morning, as soon as she awoke, she thought about him, and she was happy. And every night when she went to bed, she thought about him again, and she fell asleep smiling."

David lay quite still, except that the grip of his hand tightened slightly. His eyes never left her.

"But then, one day, he became ill," Melanie continued. "Seraphina did everything she could think of, but days passed without him getting any better. In despair she consulted an oracle. And the oracle told her, 'Your little son can only be made well in the country of Never Tell.'

"'Then I'll take him there at once,' she cried.

"But the oracle said, 'It is forbidden for such as you to go there.'

"'Then what shall I do?' she begged.

"'How much do you love your little son?' asked the oracle.

"'More than my life,' she cried.

"'Enough to give him up, and perhaps never see him again?'

"Seraphina wept, but she agreed to give up her baby to keep him alive. And that night she was visited by a shadowy figure who held out its arms without speaking. She kissed her baby goodbye, breathed a prayer for his safety and laid him in the stranger's arms. Then she covered her face, and when she looked again, she was alone.

"She went slowly into her cave, her heart breaking for the loss of her little son. And every day and every night, she thought of him, hoping he was well. Her only comfort was the thought that she'd done the best thing for him."

"What was his name?" David asked, watching her carefully.

She smiled at him. "Peter."

"And did she love him very, very much?"

"More than the whole world. But she was content never to see him, if only he could be well. When you love someone very much you want what's best for them, even if it makes you unhappy."

"And what happened? Did she ever see him again?"

"I'll tell you another night."

"But I want to know now."

Smiling, Melanie shook her head. "There's a lot more of the story to come yet." She leaned down and kissed him. "Good night, my darling. Sleep well."

His arms stole up about her neck. "Good night," he whispered, and was asleep almost at once.

"I'd better stay with him in case he awakes again," she said to Giles, and he nodded.

"I know. I can be patient. My time will come." He kissed her and slipped out.

Melanie's heart was beating with the risk she'd taken. Through the story of Seraphina she might find a way to suggest the truth to David in a form he could understand. Then perhaps he would know that his first mother had given him up from love, and stop thinking of himself as bad. Tonight had been the first step along a path that seemed filled with happiness for all three of them.

She stayed for several hours, until the grip of his hand relaxed. Only then did she creep away to her own room.

They decided to be married as soon as possible. Giles got a special license and they settled on a date two weeks ahead, in the local church, with a quiet reception at home, attended by only a few friends. Melanie did not invite her family. Her animosity had died, but they were no longer part of her life. Besides, she couldn't risk them uttering careless remarks about her past. When Giles suggested calling them, she refused so firmly that he backed off.

"I hope I never get on your wrong side," he said with a wry grin. "Beneath that sweet surface there's a touch of steel."

"All the better to protect you with," she said, touching his face lightly.

"Protect me?" he echoed in astonishment.

"Sometimes I think you need to be protected as much as David."

There was to be no honeymoon. Giles had taken as much time away from work as he dared, and neither of them wanted to leave David, who was due back at school.

Giles's happiness had transformed him, and to Melanie's loving eyes there was now no trace of the tense, brusque man that she'd first met. He even laughed and agreed when she suggested inviting the Fraynes to the wedding. Jack held no terrors for him now. Each morning he greeted her with a smiling face, and each night, when they parted, he touched her face gently, as if trying to believe that she was real. Despite the ur-

gency of their desire, David's presence had made them
agree to keep to their own rooms until after the wedding, but even without the fulfillment of passion, the
love was still there, warm and strong, and full of bright
hopes.

On the night before the wedding, Melanie put David
to bed and took up her story. "Several years passed,"
she said. "Seraphina spent them sadly, thinking about
the son she loved. Every year on Peter's birthday she
would make a cake and put candles on it to show that
he'd reached one, then two, and three, and so on."

"How old is 'so on'?" David asked, watching her
intently.

"Eight," Melanie said, and felt the little hand holding hers relax, as though this were the right answer.
"She did this for eight years." She stopped suddenly,
for something had caught in her throat at the memory
of those years. She closed her eyes, trying to fight back
the tears, but they squeezed under her eyelids and ran
down her face. Then she felt the softest possible touch
on her cheek, and when she looked, David was brushing them away.

"Go on," he whispered.

"And then one day a gray bird flew over her cave,
singing, 'I come from the land of Never Tell.' Seraphina cried, 'Do you have news of my son?' The bird
began to sing a harsh song, full of woe. 'Unhappy—
unhappy,' he cried. 'Longs for you, longs for you.'

"Seraphina said, 'Then I must go and find him. Will
you tell me where he is?' But the bird flew away crying
'Never Tell—Never Tell—Never Tell—' until his voice
faded in the distance."

Melanie stopped, for David's eyes had closed and his
breathing had become regular. She waited to make sure

that he was really asleep, then she gently freed her hand
from his, kissed her little son and crept out of the room.

Giles was standing outside. "I know what you're
trying to do," he said quietly, "but is it wise?"

"What do you mean?"

"Seraphina is supposed to be his—I won't say
'mother' because in my eyes that woman doesn't de-
serve the name. But she's the woman who gave birth to
him, isn't she? You're trying to make him feel she didn't
abandon him, but what's the point?"

"To make him feel better about her."

"But she did abandon him. Why feed him fairy tales
that will give him a false idea of her? In a few years he'll
be able to search her out for himself, and think what it'll
do to him to discover the kind of woman she really is."

"Giles, you don't know what sort of woman she really is. And I'm not concerned with a few years' time,
I'm concerned with how he feels now. Trust me."

His face broke into the loving smile that stirred her
heart. "Do whatever you think best, my darling. For
me, your goodness and truth are the fixed point in a
deceitful world."

"Giles, don't. Don't say such things. Nobody is that
good."

"You are. I've always known it."

"Don't put me on a pedestal," she begged. "I can't
live there. One day I'll come crashing off and you'll be
hurt and disillusioned."

"Never. I know you better than you know yourself."
He took her face between his hands and looked deep
into her eyes. "I can see into your soul and know that
it's beautiful. Don't try to tell me otherwise." He kissed
her tenderly. "When I think that I'm going to have you

for always I can't believe that I've been so lucky. Tell me that it's true. Tell me that you love me and always will."

"I love you," she whispered from a full heart. "I'll love you until my last breath."

"Then let it be my last breath, too, for the thought of a world without you is unbearable. Now, good night, my love. Good night for the last time. Tomorrow, and for the rest of our lives, there'll be no need to say good night."

Celia Frayne came over early to help with the last-minute preparations, and to assist the bride to dress. Her eyes lit up at the sight of Melanie's gown, made of stiff ivory silk that came to just below the knee. It was topped off by a small hat of the same material, decorated with pink rosebuds, and with the merest hint of a veil. More pink rosebuds made up the little posy Melanie would carry.

"You look glorious," she said, and sighed.

Melanie smiled at her reflection. She knew she was beautiful, but whatever the merits of the dress, her true beauty came from her joy, which beamed from her eyes and radiated from her whole being. This was her day of glory, the day she would unite herself forever with the two people she loved.

Celia had turned away to look out of the window. "There's a strange car in the drive," she said. "I wonder whose it is."

"Probably some guests came here first," Melanie said absently. She wasn't really paying attention. She'd just had the idea of going downstairs to find Giles. She was longing for the sight of his face when he saw her like this, and she felt she couldn't wait. "I'll only be a moment," she said, and slipped out.

She descended the stairs as quietly as possible, hoping to take him by surprise. The door of his study was ajar, and from inside she could hear him moving about. She crept the last few yards, took a deep breath and threw open the door. "Good morning, my love," she cried.

Then she froze on the threshold, for a tall, dark-haired woman was standing in the window bay. She had her back to the room, but Melanie knew who it was before she turned. She wanted to cry out in horror, to protest that this nightmare couldn't be happening, but her body seemed to be frozen. Before she could find her voice, the woman turned.

It was the same chilly face from eight years ago, a little harder now, a little more engraved with the lines of self-will. But still recognizably Zena.

"Darling!" Giles's voice came from close beside her. Still dazed, Melanie managed to look at him and saw with bitter irony that his face told her all that she'd hoped. He was dazzled, entranced by the sight of her, his eyes full of adoration. It was the look every bride dreamed of seeing from her groom, and in another moment his heart was going to be broken.

"Darling," he said again, his voice a caress. "You look—I can't tell you. There aren't words..." He seemed to pull himself together. "Where are my manners? This is Zena. She dropped in to return some papers of mine. Zena, this is Melanie."

A glint had appeared in Zena's eyes. "Oh, yes," she said. "I knew it was Melanie. I've heard all about you from David and from Giles, yet oddly enough it never occurred to me that you were *the* Melanie."

Giles frowned. "What do you mean? Who is *the* Melanie?"

Zena gave her a cold, poisonous smile. "Will you tell him or shall I?"

Melanie couldn't speak. Her mouth was dry. She felt as if the whole world had fallen in on her.

"Well, perhaps I'd better tell him," Zena said. "After all, you'd hardly know how to find the words to explain to Giles how you've deceived him, would you?"

"That's nonsense," Giles said at once. "I'll never believe that Melanie deceived me. Never."

"Oh, I think you will, *darling*," Zena told him brightly. "Unless, of course, she told you that she's David's natural mother. But somehow I don't think she did."

Giles gave a short, incredulous laugh. "What are you talking about, Zena?"

Zena jerked her head to Melanie, standing there as if turned to stone. "I'm talking about her, as clever a little schemer as I've ever known. She gave birth to David and signed him away to us. The day before I left for Australia she came to see me to demand him back."

Giles shook his head as if trying to clear it. "You told me David's mother didn't want him."

Zena shrugged. "She didn't, at first. She gave him up to play in a band, but then she changed her mind. If you ask me, she was unstable. I told her to get lost, and the last thing she said was that she'd get David back, no matter what she had to do. Well, now you know how far she was ready to go."

Giles turned to Melanie. "Is it true?" he asked quietly.

"It's true that I'm David's mother," she said, and saw him turn pale.

"And that—was why you took the job here?"

"Yes, but Giles, please let me—"

He silenced her, not with words but with a hand flung up as if to ward off evil. He looked from one woman to the other, frowning, slightly puzzled. With the insight of love, Melanie knew that he was trying to square this discovery with his picture of her as perfect, and a knife twisted in her heart at the thought of the misery she was bringing him.

When he spoke again his voice was under control, but the air vibrated with tension. "I think you'd better go, Zena. There can't be any more damage you want to do."

Zena picked up her purse and looked at the two of them with a sneering smile. "It's been such an enjoyable morning," she said. "I can't tell you how sick I got of hearing about the wonderful Melanie. Melanie was warm-hearted, Melanie was honest, Melanie knew how to play games with children, Melanie was everything I wasn't. Well, now you know the truth about your precious Melanie. She's been stringing you along from the start, with just one aim in view. Did you think she loved you, Giles? Well, that may be what she told you, but there's only one person she loves, and we have it from her own lips that she'd do anything to get him. Goodbye."

Neither of the others paid her any heed as she departed. They stood staring at each other as the front door slammed and the world disintegrated around them. Giles looked like a man in a state of shock. It was Melanie who found her voice first.

"Giles, please—don't judge me without hearing my side," she begged.

"I thought I'd just heard it."

"Zena's version. She lied to you about me, telling you that I gave David up heartlessly, when she knew I wanted him back. You've believed that lie all these years."

"Yes, she lied to me. But she's not the only one, is she?"

"I couldn't tell you who I was when I came here," she said passionately. "You'd have thrown me out, as she did. I just wanted to see David and be near him. I was sixteen when he was born. I wanted to keep him, but Oliver ran off when he knew I was pregnant, and everyone kept on at me to give my baby up for his sake. My family wouldn't help me. It broke my heart to let him go, but I did it. I had postpartum depression—I hardly knew what I was doing. And then it was too late. I wanted him back but I'd signed the papers."

"How did you know who had him?"

"A friend on the council told me. I confronted Zena in this very house, but it was no use. She took him abroad and I lost track of him until a few months ago. When I found him in that school—"

"You laid your plans," Giles said, speaking in a quiet, stunned manner that unnerved her. "Yes, I can see how it must have been."

"The only plan I laid was to be with him. When I learned that Zena had gone, and how unhappy he was, I knew he needed me. I'm his mother. What else could I do?"

"Nothing, I suppose," he said in a voice that was almost normal. For a moment hope lived in her, but his next words killed it. "Of course you wanted to get him back. And if in the process you had to lie and cheat and deceive the fool who was falling in love with you, well, so what? Motherhood is a ruthless business, after all."

"Giles, please—"

"I should have known from the start, shouldn't I? Looking back, I can see that the signs were always there. You hated me that first day. You kept it under control, but you hated me. I was the enemy, wasn't I? *Wasn't I?*"

The sudden rage, coming out of nowhere, made her flinch. Her mouth felt dry. "I thought so," she said, and choked. "But I didn't know you then."

"You played me beautifully, like a fish on the end of a line. I could almost admire you for it. Only one person has ever deceived me so totally before—I told you about him, didn't I? But you had an advantage. I wanted to believe in you. My God, how I wanted it! So I closed my eyes to all the things that should have warned me. The way you wouldn't go near Zena, too afraid she'd recognize you. You wouldn't even give David your picture for the visit, in case she saw it. Oh, yes, you were careful, but you slipped up, as well. You knew about Australia, when you shouldn't have done.

"And the color of your hair. It's not a common shade, and David's inherited it from you, but even then I didn't suspect, blind fool that I was, because I thought you were incapable of deceit. Oh, I fell for it hook, line and sinker. When did you decide that you'd be safer if you married me? Not long after, I'll bet."

"No, it wasn't like that!" she cried. "When I knew I was falling in love with you I drew back at first because I felt so guilty about deceiving you."

"Then why deceive me?" he ask coldly. "You've had enough chances to tell me the truth."

"I was afraid to in case you sent me away."

"Ah, yes, away from David."

"And from you."

"Oh, no." He raised his hand in the same gesture as before, as though defending himself from her. "Let's have no more of that. It was a good line and it's served its purpose. It took me in long enough to get me to the wedding day."

"It's the truth," she said wildly.

"You said it yourself. You'd get David back, whatever you had to do—"

"That was years ago. I'm a different person."

"But you're not. You came here with one thing fixed in your sights—David. That hasn't changed, and neither have you. What bad luck that Zena walked in when she did."

Melanie paled. "Giles, don't send me away, please. Whatever I've done, you couldn't be that cruel."

"Do you think you have the right to lecture me about cruelty?" he demanded coldly.

"Maybe not. I never meant to hurt you—I could still make you happy—"

"Never." The word burst from him with explosive force.

"If you won't marry me, let me stay in my old job. I'll scrub floors, anything. You need never see me. But don't send me away from David, I beg you."

His face was stone. "I never want to set eyes on your scheming, deceitful face again. I never want to hear your name again. I'll forget you, and I'll make my son forget you."

She gave a cry of agony and dropped her face into her hands. The pain wasn't just for herself and David, so soon to be parted again. It was for Giles, too. His expression was that of the man he'd been when she first came here: the tense, mistrustful man, lost in a desert of confusion and emptiness. She'd led him out of that dreadful place, only to send him back. It would be worse now that he'd glimpsed happiness and lost it. His suspicious nature would grow harder, and he would pass it on to David. And she, who loved them more than life, had done this to them.

She raised her head to make one final plea, but before she could speak, she heard David's voice in the hall. She turned frantic eyes on Giles and saw his own answering desperation. Before either of them could speak, David had pushed open the door and run into the office.

"Mommy was here," he said urgently. "I saw her car." He looked around the room, and his face settled into the old lines of rigid despair as he realized Zena wasn't there. "She's gone. She didn't come to see me." The urgency had drained from his voice, leaving it flat and resigned.

Giles gave a slight shudder, and with an effort wiped everything from his face but concern for his son. "She—she would have liked to see you—but she was in a rush.... " His voice fell away lamely.

Then, to their astonishment, the despair left David's face, and he smiled. "It doesn't matter," he said simply.

Giles stared. "Doesn't it?"

David turned to Melanie. He seemed to have grown several years. This was no longer an eight-year-old child, but a young man who'd accepted the pain of life and learned to counter it with the good. "It doesn't matter now," he said. "We've got Melanie instead."

She couldn't speak, but he didn't seem to need any answer. It was as if he'd settled things in his own mind. He picked up her bouquet, which had fallen to the floor. "You dropped this," he said worriedly. "But it's

all right. There's only a few flowers which are spoiled."
He pulled one out. "There. Nobody will know it's not
perfect, will they?"

"No," Melanie said, dazed. "Nobody will know it's
not perfect—except us." She was watching Giles.

David slipped his hand confidingly in hers. "And
when you've married Daddy, you're going to be with us
forever and ever, aren't you?"

Melanie met Giles's eyes, daring him to deny her.
"Yes," she said. "When I've married Daddy, I'm going to be with you forever and ever."

Giles didn't move. He seemed transfixed by the sight
of Melanie, standing there with David's hand in hers,
the child's face glowing with renewed happiness and
confidence.

"Yes," he said heavily at last. "That's how it will
be."

Melanie was never able to remember her wedding in
any detail, although moments of it stood out from the
mist. The walk down the aisle on Jack Frayne's arm,
Giles growing nearer. She'd dreamed of seeing him
watch her approach with a look of love, but all she
could discern on his face now was a frozen determination to hide all emotion. That look stayed in place as he
promised to love and cherish her. Only once did it alter
by a fraction, when the priest asked Melanie if she
would live "forsaking all others, keep thee only unto
him." A look of perceptible irony hovered on his lips
for a brief moment, and then was gone.

When he placed the wedding ring on her finger, his
hands were as cold as ice, but no colder than his lips
when he bestowed the obligatory kiss on her.

Then the car journey home, the two of them alone in the back, save for the chauffeur cut off by a pane of glass. She turned to him, longing to see some softening in his face, but there was only a mocking smile on his lips as he said, "You're a very clever woman, Melanie. A determined one, too, but it's the sheer ruthless cunning that inspires my awe."

And that was all he said to her as they drove back from their wedding.

Ten

The reception was even worse. Jack made a speech, telling the audience how he'd met Giles and Melanie in Italy.

"And I knew something was going on," he said cheerfully, "because when I dared to ask Melanie straight out if she was in love with Giles, she said 'Nonsense!' so firmly that it was obvious wedding bells couldn't be far off."

The guests laughed as they were meant to, but under the table Melanie clenched her hands, knowing how this story would seem to Giles.

It was David who made the terrible day bearable. He was sitting next to her, and from time to time she could feel his hand slip into hers as if seeking reassurance. She squeezed him back, smiling. She'd done what she'd always longed to do. She'd got her son back. But her heart was heavy.

When the meal was over and she was circulating among the guests, Jack drew her aside. "You didn't mind my telling that story, did you?" he asked. "It was obvious that the two of you were crazy about each other, even then."

"Was it?" she asked wistfully.

Giles came up to them. "I must thank you, Frayne," he said to Jack. "An excellent speech. Most illuminating."

Jack seemed to become aware of seething undercurrents, and, being an uncomplicated young man, hastily changed the subject. "By the way, what's the name of your son?" he demanded.

"David," Melanie said. "You know that from the holiday."

"Well, I thought I did, but I've just heard him introducing himself to someone as Peter. Why would he do that?"

"It's a child's fantasy game," Melanie said quickly. "You know what they're like at that age."

Someone claimed Jack's attention, leaving her with Giles. "So it worked, *Seraphina*," he said softly. "My God, you laid your plans cleverly. Everything has panned out just the way you meant. My congratulations."

"No, Giles—" But he'd already turned away and was laughing with his guests like the happiest bridegroom in the world.

At last everyone was gone, and they were alone. David threw his arms around Melanie and gave her a bear hug, which she returned eagerly. "Time you were in bed, young man," she said.

When he was tucked up, he begged, "Tell me some more about Seraphina and Peter. Did she go to the land of Never Tell?"

She knew now that David was identifying with Peter, and at any other time she would have seized on her victory. Tonight all she wanted was to go to Giles and find some way to make it right. But David had to come first, and so she settled on the bed and began to talk in a dreamy, faraway voice. "Yes, Seraphina set out for the land of Never Tell. At last she reached the border and there her way was barred by a shadow. 'Go back,' he said in a hoarse whisper. 'You are forbidden to enter here.'

"But Seraphina implored him to let her pass. 'I must find my son,' she said. 'For I love him more than anything in life.'

"Then the shadow took pity on her, and whispered, 'Because you love so much, I will allow you to enter for one day. But then you must be gone.' Seraphina thanked him, and entered the land of Never Tell.

"It was a strange place, and she wandered here and there, calling Peter's name. But she heard nothing. At last she came to a pool of clear water. She looked in and spread her hands in a magical gesture, saying, 'Let me see my son as he is now.' And as she looked, the reflection of a little boy appeared in the water beside her."

"What did he look like?" David asked eagerly.

"He was eight years old and he had fair hair," Melanie said, brushing her hand against a stray lock of David's hair and smiling.

"What color was Seraphina's hair?" David persisted.

"It was exactly the same color."

"What did they do?"

"They looked at their reflections in the water, and smiled, for they knew each other. Seraphina cried, 'Where are you?' But instead of answering, he vanished."

"And what happened then?" David demanded.

"That's something I'll tell you another night," Melanie said, smiling.

"Oh, no, *please*. I want to know now."

But Melanie shook her head. How could she tell him how the story ended when she didn't know herself? "Go to sleep," she said, and kissed him. David snuggled down without further protest, and was asleep in seconds.

This was her wedding night, when her groom should have been eagerly waiting to take her into his arms for the consummation of their love. Instead she found their bedroom empty and Giles's wedding suit crumpled on the floor, as though he'd tossed it away from him in a rage.

She stood still for a moment, her heart sinking. How could she reach this difficult man whose heart had opened to her, only to flinch back on itself at the discovery of her deception?

She went quietly downstairs. The study door was shut forbiddingly against her, and it took all her courage to walk across and open it. Giles was sitting at his desk, apparently absorbed in some paperwork. He didn't look up.

"Giles," she said gently, "we can't leave it like this. We have to talk."

At last he raised his head and she nearly cried out at the sight of his face. He'd aged since the morning. Lines of strain had settled around his mouth and his eyes seemed to be sunk in shadow. "Is there anything to talk about?" he inquired distantly.

"Of course there is. Surely you can at least listen to me before judging me?"

"I thought I had listened to you, this morning," Giles said, his voice like an arctic wind. "Afterward I told you I wasn't impressed by your excuses. In fact I distinctly remember saying that I never wanted to see or hear from you again. But you found a way to make me do what you wanted anyway. Which, of course, is what you've always done. I'm impressed. It's lucky you don't go into business, or, with your cunning and ability to manipulate the enemy, you'd bankrupt the rest of us."

"Don't speak of yourself as the enemy," she said passionately. "You're the man I love."

"Oh, please," he said wearily. "I'm the man you made use of to get what you wanted, and very cleverly."

"*Giles—*"

"I see all your arguments, and they're good ones. He was your son. *Yours.* The fact that you signed him away was neither here nor there. Never let feeble considerations of natural justice distract you when you've decided that you want something. It's a code I live by myself. I have no complaints about your using it."

"How dare you say I signed him away!" she exploded.

"Didn't you?"

"I gave him up for his own good and regretted it ever after. I told you that this morning."

"You said anything that would serve your purpose this morning."

"But it's true," she said wildly. "I've grieved for David for eight years. I've kept his birthday every year—"

"And bought him gifts, and dreamed of the day you'd get him back," he said with a sneer. "Yes, I've heard the story of Seraphina. A brilliant strategy."

"The only strategy was to make David realize that his natural mother didn't abandon him callously, that she did it out of love. I'm trying to save him from feeling that his mother never loved him. You of all people should understand why."

Before her eyes, his face changed terribly, and a bleak, withered look overtook it. "I only needed you to remind me of that," he said softly. "Something that I confided to you and to nobody else in the world. My God, when I think of the things I told you, the way I trusted you—what a fool I was! So naively certain that I could read you easily, and find only sweetness and truth. How you must have laughed!"

"You know better," she said. "There were times when we—when you know I wasn't laughing."

"If you don't mind I'd rather not think of that."

"Well, I do mind," she said angrily. "Those were the times we were closest, when you knew me best, and if you ignore them then you're shutting out my best hope of convincing you."

"Convincing me of what?"

"That I love you."

"Spare yourself the effort. You have no hope of ever convincing me of that. As for knowing you and being close to you, I'm not fool enough to imagine that we knew each other merely because we shared sex, and you shouldn't be, either."

"Shared sex!" she cried. "How dare you say that! It was more than sex and you know it."

"You don't understand, Melanie," he said softly. "It's only by telling myself that those moments were no more than the gratification of lust that I can bear the sight of you. If I allowed myself to remember what I felt then—what I believed—that I loved you and thought you loved me—if I started remembering that, then I should hate you with all my soul."

"How can you hate me when I love you so much?"

"Stop it!" he said fiercely.

"I won't stop it. I want you to remember what happened between us. Think about it. Let your heart remember, as well as your body, and you'll know it wasn't just sex. It wasn't for me, and I don't believe it was for you."

"Then believe it." Giles gave a bitter laugh. "What makes you think your body's any different than other women's?"

"It's different for you. I know it is. I know you've held me as you've never held anyone else. I know you've touched and caressed me with a tenderness no other woman has known. I know you love me, and I won't let you deny it."

She was stopped by the sound of his hand crashing down on the desk. "That's enough," he shouted. "You've had your victory. A decent woman would have left it there. But you're not a decent woman, you're a predator who has to have the satisfaction of the kill every time. I could have forgiven you wanting David at any cost, even if I was the victim. Motherhood is a human instinct, and if it's ruthless it's because it has to be.

"But you want more, don't you? You need to get me back at your feet, singing hymns to your truth and honesty, the way I used to. It's not enough to have made a fool of me once. You want to prove you can do it again. What kind of kick does that give you?"

"Giles, please—don't do this."

He didn't hear her. He was possessed by rage and a kind of self-loathing. "And it would be a victory, wouldn't it? Fooling me the first time was easy. I was off guard, and besides, I handed you all the weapons. But fooling me again, when I'm on the watch for you, that would be a real triumph. You told me yourself, you hated me."

"Only at first."

"I wonder. I had David for those first eight years. You must have built up a splendid hatred of me during that time, and you worked out the perfect revenge. . . ." He stopped and a shudder went through him. Melanie reached out in pity for his torment, but he held her off. His brow was damp from the effort at control.

"Don't touch me," he warned. "Just—don't—touch—me."

Cornered, she went onto the attack. "Why?" she flung at him. "What are you afraid of if I touch you? That it's not as simple as you try to make out? That there's more between us than you want to pretend?"

"Are you going to lecture me about pretense?" he asked with grim humor. "I warn you, don't."

"I did what I had to. But on the way I fell in love with you. I didn't want to, but I did. After that it was complicated."

"Not for you, surely? A mind like a steel trap, capable of calculating anything—what could be complicated?"

She knew that he was attacking her out of the bottomless depths of his hurt, but it was terrible all the same. There seemed no way to reach him, but she made one last try. "Don't shut me out, Giles, please. Not for my sake, but for your own—and David's."

"You got that in the wrong order."

"No, I didn't. David's going to be all right now, but you won't be, not if you hide yourself away in some cold desert where I can't find you."

He viewed her ironically. "The beauty of a cold desert is that you know exactly where you are. Take it from a man who's lived in one. Never mind me. Just think of David. He won't suffer. As far as he knows, everything will be fine between us."

"You underestimate him. He'll see through that."

"We'll have to make sure he doesn't. The line is drawn in the sand, Melanie. There's no going beyond it now."

"The line will never be drawn," she said passionately. "I won't let you draw it with you on one side and me on the other."

His mouth twisted in a sneer. "Would it really thrill you to hear me say that I still want you? All right, I'll say it. You want to know that I lie awake at night thinking of holding your naked body against me? Fine. Consider it said. And the way you move against me, and whisper my name, and know how to make me think I'm pleasing you—"

"You do please me," she said huskily. "I want that, and I want to please you. Let me please you, Giles."

He stood, stony eyed, looking at her. He didn't move when Melanie touched his face gently, but his burning eyes searched her. Taking hope from his stillness, she laid her lips against his and began to move them softly. "Let me please you," she whispered.

She could feel his tension as he strove to resist her. She fought him with all the weapons at her command, with the little teasing movements that she knew delighted him, with the warm urgency of her body, but most of all with her love. Her love cried out to him in silence, imploring him to understand and forgive, and to let her free him from the darkness that could so easily claim him again.

He raised his hands and seized her arms, as if to throw her off, but it seemed as if he couldn't do it, for instead of pushing her away he tightened his grip. For a moment he stood rigid, motionless, while the battle raged this way and that. Then, with a groan, he seized her in a rough embrace. The kiss changed, became his kiss, fierce, demanding. She yielded to it eagerly, parting her lips in invitation.

Barely waiting for her response, he drove his tongue roughly into her mouth. It was different now, with none of the flickering movements with which he'd teased her in the past. He was no longer evoking her response, but demanding it.

She thought she understood. He wanted the reassurance of feeling her passion. It was a reassurance she could give easily, for her whole body was flooded by desire for him. If she could only be one with him now, their troubles would melt in the white heat of physical love.

She exerted all her skill to show how much she wanted him. With her mouth still locked on his, she began to tear open the buttons of his shirt and run her hands over his chest, using the little caresses that she knew he loved. The result was explosive. A groan was torn from his depths. He wrenched the shirt off and tossed it to the floor. His hands twined in her tumbled hair, pulling her against him. He kissed her frantically with lips that burned and demanded. The next moment he was ripping her dress. The beautiful silk disintegrated and fell to the floor. Melanie had meant to treasure her wedding dress all her life, but she let it go without a regret. It was worth any sacrifice to win Giles back.

She had a glimpse of his face, the eyes blurred with passion, lit from within by a fierce glow. Then he crushed her mouth again with a kiss that set her afire. His passion had a ruthless edge that was unfamiliar, but she responded to it with a new rush of excitement. She loved Giles for his tenderness when she was in his arms, but their past lovemaking had been a journey that left her ready for this new, more vigorous experience. She helped him to throw off the rest of her clothes, and then his own.

Then she was lying on the sofa, the feel of the silky soft leather against her back, pulling him eagerly down on top of her. "I'm yours, Giles," she breathed. "I want you to be mine—all mine—"

"I know," he growled. "I know—you want—everything."

"Yes," she whispered against his mouth. *"Everything."*

He responded by driving into her without preliminaries. She gasped at the sheer piercing force of pleasure that was renewed again and again with every rhythmic thrust. She cried out his name in a mixture of plea and affirmation, holding him close in a union so furnace-hot that it seemed to her they were fused in one perfect whole. She was consumed by pleasure, possessed by it, renewed by it. As she arched convulsively against him she touched the stars, bringing them raining down on her in an extravaganza of delight.

It was all hers again, she thought in wonder. Every beautiful thing they'd shared had been given back to her, with all its promise for the future. As her body grew calmer and her heart slowed its thunder she gave a sigh of happiness and opened her eyes.

What she saw made her stiffen with horror. Giles was looking at her with the closed face of a stranger. It was the face she'd seen when she'd found him here tonight, but now it was harder, colder, more unforgiving. Everything she'd thought had happened had been an illusion.

"Very well," he grated. "You did what you wanted to do. You proved that you can still make me want your clever body. Are you pleased now? Can't you understand that your body is nothing? It was your heart I wanted, until I found how ruthless and manipulative it was. And if I had any doubts about that you've just dispelled them. I wonder if you'll feel your victory was worth it when you understand that by making me despise myself you've also made me des—"

"No," she whispered, putting a hand over his mouth. "Don't say it."

"I don't need to say it. You know." He rose from the sofa, returned to the desk and seated himself behind it. "Would you mind leaving me now? I have rather a lot of work to do."

Eleven

Giles was about to start a meeting in the boardroom when the phone rang.

"Mr. Haverill? This is Mrs. Grady, David's headmistress. I'm afraid he's had an accident."

"What kind of accident?" he demanded sharply. "How bad?"

"He was hit by a car. The ambulance is on its way. I've tried to contact Mrs. Haverill, but there's no reply."

"She's out," Giles said. "I'll call her on the car phone."

He noted the name of the hospital and slammed down the receiver. "I'm sorry, gentlemen. The meeting is canceled."

"But we were going to discuss the Haydock contract," his assistant complained. "It's important."

"Haydock be damned, and his contract be damned with him," Giles snapped. "My son is important."

He called Melanie's car phone and told her what had happened. He heard her gasp at the other end, and when she spoke again her voice was husky, but she was steady. "I'll be there," she said when he gave her the hospital name. "But Giles, I'm out of town at that big complex. It'll take me at least half an hour to get there. Tell David—tell him I'm hurrying."

When she'd hung up he stared at the phone, wondering what he'd expected: pleas for his support? Tears? Not now. He knew he'd pushed her too far away from him for that.

In the month since their marriage he'd maintained a distant courtesy, smiling in front of David, but otherwise avoiding her. They shared a room, to keep up the pretense for David, but often he worked late, sometimes not returning home until the small hours. He told himself how glad she must be of his absence that gave her the chance to be with her son. On the odd occasions when they happened to retire at the same time, they lay far apart, a terrible silence between them.

One evening he'd stood at the downstairs window, watching her romping with David. To his hungry eyes they seemed encircled by a golden aureole that excluded outsiders. After a while he'd entered by the front door and gone straight to his office. When Melanie looked in, he'd asked for coffee and sandwiches, but hadn't spoken of what he'd seen.

As he drove to the hospital he argued with himself, vainly seeking reassurance. It simply wasn't possible that David could die now, not after everything they'd all been through. But there in his mind all the time was a vision of Melanie's face, if she lost her child, the one person in the world she cared about. She would have nothing else to live for. Giles knew that he alone would be no consolation for her.

At the hospital a nurse directed him to the corridor outside David's room, but once there Giles stiffened with outrage at what he saw. "You!" he said with loathing to Mrs. Braddock. "I might have known you wouldn't pass up the chance to make trouble."

But his voice faded as Mrs. Braddock lifted her head. She looked ghastly. "I know what you're thinking," she said in a voice barely above a whisper. "And you're wrong. I'm not here to make trouble. It—it was my fault."

"What do you mean?" he demanded.

Mrs. Grady, the headmistress, rose and faced them. "Mrs. Braddock came to the school to see David. I'm afraid he didn't want to see her, and ran away."

"And that's how he came to be out on the street?" Giles demanded. "How bad is he?"

At that moment a grave, bearded man appeared and introduced himself as Dr. Carter. He spoke kindly, but no amount of kindness could soften what he had to say. "David has lost a lot of blood," he said. "We've stabilized him, but we need to operate. Unfortunately his blood group is AB negative, which is rare, and our stocks of that type are very low. I've put out a call for emergency supplies, but until they arrive I daren't even start. I understand that David is your adoptive son?"

"Yes."

"It's a pity. If you and your wife had been his natural parents we might have—"

"My wife is his natural mother," Giles said bluntly.

He wasn't aware of Mrs. Grady's start of surprise, or of Mrs. Braddock's mouth dropping. He knew now why fate had brought Melanie into his life.

Dr. Carter nodded. "That will help. Will she be here soon?"

"She has some distance to travel, but she's on her way. I want to see David," Giles stated.

"Of course. This way."

Giles thought of himself as strong, but he felt sick at the mass of tubes attached to David. The little boy lay in the center of the white bed, his face blanched almost to the color of the pillow. He looked small and very frail.

Giles drew up a chair and sat beside the bed, taking the small hand gently into his. After a while David opened his eyes, and murmured, "Hello, Daddy."

"Hello, old son." He tried to keep his voice steady.

"Is Mommy here?"

"Mommy" had always been Zena. David had always called Melanie by her name, but Giles took a chance and said, "She'll be here soon."

David didn't answer. His eyes had closed again. Giles bent his head and prayed as he'd never prayed in his life. Let his son live. Let Melanie arrive quickly. Let her coming make everything all right. Let her turn to him for comfort.

Minutes passed. David awoke again and murmured drowsily. "Is she coming?"

And Giles answered, "Yes, she's coming. Hold on to me."

He felt the slight pressure from the little hand, and squeezed back. But he knew it wasn't enough. Melanie was the one David wanted and needed.

At last he heard footsteps outside, then the door opened and Melanie appeared, going straight to the bed. David smiled feebly. "Hello, Mommy," he whispered.

Her returning smile was glowing, as though she hadn't a care in the world. Nobody could have guessed her anguish, Giles thought. Nothing mattered but to strengthen and reassure her child.

Dr. Carter appeared. "Mrs. Haverill, do you know your blood group?" he asked urgently.

"Yes. I'm AB negative."

"Thank God! Then we're in business. I'll need some of your blood on standby in case David needs a transfusion. I'll take a sample to start with."

Things began to move fast. Giles watched silently as Melanie offered her hand for the pinprick. Dr. Carter called the operating theater and briskly told them to make ready. The machine for taking Melanie's blood was wheeled in so that she could give it without leaving David. Giles stayed at the bedside, holding David's hand, but the child's face was turned the other way, to where he could keep his eyes on Melanie.

Giles watched the container fill with the red liquid, the stuff of life that was going to save his son. No, not his son. Hers. He'd known it before, but only in his head. Now it was real. This, in the end, was what life was about. He could plan David's future and give him every advantage. He could love him with all his heart. But it was her blood that flowed in the child's veins, not his own.

"I'm going to stop there," Dr. Carter said.

"Have you got all you need?" Melanie asked.

"Well, a little more would help, but I have to think of you, as well—"

"Take as much as you need," she said firmly. "That's all that matters."

"All right. Just a little more." The doctor turned to Giles. "Would you like to explain to David about the preop injection?"

Giles nodded and David turned to him. "The nurse is going to give you an injection, to send you to sleep," he said. "It's nothing to worry about, and when you wake up you'll feel a lot better."

"Is Mommy going to be all right?"

"Yes, she's fine. Don't worry about a thing."

The little boy hardly seemed to notice the prick of the needle, and a few moments later his eyelids began to droop. Melanie climbed carefully down from the couch where she'd been lying and bent over to kiss David. His eyes opened briefly, he smiled at her and she smiled back. Giles stood by the wall, a solitary, excluded figure. At last the trolley moved off, Melanie with it, still holding David's hand.

Giles went out into the corridor. Mrs. Grady and Mrs. Braddock were still there. Mrs. Braddock was haggard. "Is that true?" she asked faintly, "about your wife being David's mother?"

"Perfectly true," Giles told her. "She's just given her blood, which matches his as no other woman's could."

"But how—?"

"Does it matter?" Giles asked wearily. "Does anything count except that she's the only person who can save his life?" He added, half to himself, "What else matters but that?"

He found his way to the operating theater. Melanie would be sitting outside and in their shared anguish he might find a way to take her hand. His rage against her had evaporated. Now he could think only of her pain

and how he might help it. But at the same time he knew
there was no consolation she could find in him. He was
nothing to her.

There was no sign of her outside the operating theater. Just an empty corridor and empty chairs. A nurse
he'd seen before emerged from the theater and he asked
about Melanie.

"Your wife went to the chapel," she said gently. "It's
just down there, on the right."

He found the little chapel. Pushing open the door, he
saw Melanie kneeling in a pew close to the altar. Her
head was buried in her hands and she seemed oblivious
to everything. He longed to go and kneel beside her, to
join his prayers to hers and let her know that what hurt
her also hurt him. But it was too late. He'd driven her
too far away. He knew that now.

He waited, hoping she would turn and he would see
in her eyes the need that would help him approach her.
But she never moved and at last, sick at heart, he closed
the door and went away.

Kneeling in the chapel, Melanie was intensely aware
of everything that was around her. Even the silence
seemed to have a vibrant quality.

Her prayers had begun as words, but the words had
dissolved into an incoherent plea that her son might be
saved. As time passed, that too became less definite and
changed into the picture of David's face, smiling, as so
often it was these days. She knew that the deity she believed in would understand that in her distraught and
weakened state these images were the only form of
prayer she could manage. She felt as though she were
laying David in arms powerful enough to heal him, and

saying, "See how beautiful he is. Don't take him from me."

Suddenly, in her mind, Giles was there beside his son: Giles as he'd once been, looking at her with love, not the distant stranger she'd known since their marriage. Then his face changed. The joy drained from it, leaving behind not anger but desolation. This was Giles as he would look when he was bereft, when his son's love, the only kind that hadn't betrayed him, was snatched away. Her heart ached for him more than herself, and she longed to reach out to him in comfort.

Her heightened senses told her the moment when the door opened behind her, and she knew that it was Giles who stood there. In another moment he would come to her and their mutual love for their son would end hostility and perhaps allow their love for each other to flow freely again. She waited, while the silence seemed to vibrate around her. Then she heard the faint click of the door closing, and when she looked around she found herself alone. At last she rose wearily and went to the door. But the corridor outside was empty, and she knew that her hope had been in vain.

The operation took three hours. When it was over the surgeon came out smiling. "Went like a dream," he said in a cheerful staccato. "Had to give him a transfusion. Took it well. Not expecting any problems now. You go home and get some rest."

"No, I shall stay here," Melanie insisted at once.

"So shall I," Giles said.

But he wasn't given the chance. His assistant, unable to contact him on the mobile phone that he'd switched off, came hurrying to the hospital. When he heard that the news about David was good, he plunged into a series of urgent messages, evidently assuming that since he was dealing with Giles Haverill, work should take priority.

"Look, can't this wait?" Giles said impatiently. "I switched the phone off because I wanted to be left alone."

"It's all right," Melanie said calmly. "Why don't you get back to work?"

He was about to protest that he would stay with her when he saw the remoteness in her eyes and realized, like a blow in the stomach, that she was glad of the excuse to be rid of him. "Very well," he said curtly. "In that case I'll go."

He strode to the end of the corridor. There he looked back in case she was following him with her eyes. But a nurse was showing her into David's room and, while Giles watched, the door closed behind her.

She moved into the hospital that same day, sleeping in David's room and helping the nurses as far as they would let her. David's recovery was swift. Once he'd come through the operation he regained strength rapidly.

He began to receive visitors. Mrs. Wade came, bringing Sylvia, who promptly demanded to see his operation scar. When David proudly displayed it, she loftily asserted that she'd seen one *much* bigger than that. David indignantly insisted that she hadn't and in the riotous argument that followed he became almost his old self.

"I'm sorry," Mrs. Wade said nervously, hauling her unruly charge out of the room. "I should have made her behave."

She had to raise her voice to be heard above Sylvia yelling "Have, have, *have*" over her shoulder.

"Haven't, haven't, *haven't,*" David shouted back.

"Don't worry," Melanie said, also raising her voice. "I haven't heard him laugh so much since he's been in here."

Mrs. Braddock came, too, not to see David but Melanie. She looked older. "I thought you'd like to know that I've sent in a report saying David's problems have been resolved satisfactorily," she said. "You'll have no more trouble."

"Thank you." Melanie spoke coolly, but the other woman's misery gave her a twinge of sympathy. She wouldn't let her see David for fear of upsetting him, but she bought her a cup of tea and sent her away more cheerful.

Giles visited every evening and Melanie left them alone together. Afterward she would chat to David until it was time for him to go to sleep. Every night he demanded to know more about Seraphina and her search for her son. It was obvious that on some deep, instinctive level he knew what she was trying to convey to him, but they never spoke of it openly. It was as though a fragile web of communication were being spun between them, and a blunt word could destroy its subtle beauty.

Melanie was drawing the story out. It would have been simple to reunite the fictional mother and son, as had happened in real life, but she was reluctant to do this. Until things became right between her and Giles, there was something missing in her own life and in Seraphina's life. So she filled in with incidental adventures, waiting for the moment when she would find out how everything ended.

She knew Giles sometimes stood in the corridor, listening, and she started to leave the door ajar so that he could hear better. She longed for him to come in and join them, but he never did, and her heart ached to think how isolated he must feel, just when he'd thought he'd found love.

Usually he would slip away as soon as she'd finished, but one night he stayed and said quietly, "Tell me about this witch. Could she do black magic?"

"No," Melanie said at once. "She was a good witch. She made mistakes, but they were the mistakes of love."

"She loved her son, and she'd sacrifice anyone for him, wouldn't she? I have no complaints."

"Haven't you?" she asked.

"You did what you had to. You're his mother. I understand that now in a way I didn't before. I have no right to blame you for anything you did to get him back. I know I said these things on our wedding day, but I said them in bitterness. I'm not sure how much I really meant, and how much was just a way to attack you. But it's different now."

"Is it?" she said hopefully.

"I mean I see things more clearly. When you told the doctor to take as much of your blood as he needed— you'd have given every last drop to save David, wouldn't you?"

"Yes. But then, so would you. I know that."

"But I couldn't," he said simply. "My blood is useless to him. All the adoption papers in the world won't create the bond that's between parent and child. A man can't fight against that, and I was a fool to try."

"Giles, please, if we both love him so much, can't we—?" She stopped, beaten back by the remoteness in his eyes.

"We can do what's best for him," Giles said. "We can love him, and forget about ourselves. I don't know what we might have had—perhaps nothing. Perhaps everything. But I know it's too late now. I won't make your life hard, Melanie. Just look after Peter—I mean, David.''

He pressed her hand. It was the nearest thing to a sign of warmth that he'd given her since their wedding. She would have reached out to him, but he turned quickly and walked away. Melanie went into David's room. The lights were out except for a small one beside the bed, and she crossed over to the window, from where she had a view of the parking lot. After a moment Giles came in sight, walking to the far end where his car was parked. She watched him as his figure became smaller, and thought that she'd never seen a man who looked more lonely.

Twelve

The day after David's return home, Giles explained that he must leave immediately on a trip that had been too long delayed. "I didn't want to go until he was safely home," he said. "But now—"

"It was good of you to wait so long," she said politely. "David and I will be fine now. I hope you have a successful trip."

"Thank you."

That was how it was between them now: painful courtesy, consideration for each other's feelings, eyes carefully not meeting.

He was away for a fortnight. He returned laden with orders that kept him late at work most nights. When he did return, he spent the evenings shut up in his private office.

One evening while he was there the phone rang, not his mobile but the house phone. He lifted the receiver and found himself talking to the desk sergeant at the local police station. Giles recognized him as the one who'd been on duty the night David was taken there. "We've got a drunk in the cells," the sergeant told him. "We can't get his name out of him, and he's too far gone to make any sense. But he keeps saying your name over and over, and he's got a photograph that looks like your son. Could you come and see if you can identify him?"

"I'll be right down."

He told Melanie that he had to go out for a while. He didn't say where and she didn't ask. He hurried to the police station. There the sergeant showed him into an interview room where the drunk sat, lolling against the wall, regarding the world with a jaundiced eye that sharpened to hatred when he saw Giles.

"No, I've never seen this man," Giles said, looking at him with distaste.

"You don't remember me, do you?" the drunk raged. "You wreck my life and you don't even remember me." His voice rose. "But I was gonna pay it back— I was—if I'd had the chance—I was gonna—" He faded out in a mumble.

"Oh, yes, now I recall you," Giles said in disgust. "Oliver Dane. You had your fingers in the till of a company I was looking at."

"It's a lie," the man said thickly. "I was gonna pay— I was— "

Giles turned to the sergeant. "What's this about my son's photograph?" He stared at the picture of a little boy in a striped sweater that the sergeant put into his hands. "Can you leave me alone with him?" he asked at last.

When the door was shut on them, he turned to Oliver Dane, who flinched before the terrible look in Giles's eyes. "You have five seconds to tell me how you come to have David's picture," he said.

"That's not David," Oliver whined.

"Do you expect me to believe—?" Giles's voice faded as he looked at the picture again, noticing slight but significant differences. It wasn't David, but someone so like him that the hairs began to rise on the back of his neck. Now he knew where he'd heard the name Oliver before. Melanie had let slip that Oliver—

"Who is this?" he asked through a dry throat.

"My younger brother, Phil," Oliver said. "Taken years ago—"

Giles fought for calm. "And how does your brother come to look so much like my son?"

Oliver gave a wheezy laugh, blasting Giles with whiskey fumes. "My son," he whispered. *"My* son. And wouldn't you like to know who his mother is?"

"I already do," Giles said coldly.

Oliver's face distorted with hate. "Bitch! Stupid bitch! I told her—warned her—we could have had everything—"

Giles took his collar none too gently. "Are you telling me that you've spoken to her recently?" he demanded through gritted teeth.

"'Course I have—followed her—caught up with her one day. Lord, you should have seen her face!" He took a deep breath and spoke with concentrated effort. "I had it all planned—her and me—natural parents—that Braddock woman would have given David to us. And you—you'd have been paid back for what you did to me."

Giles released him. He was fighting not to let this loathsome creature see that he was shaking. "What a neat plan! Why didn't it come off?"

Oliver's face twisted with hate. "Because the stupid bitch wouldn't help me. I told her—she could have him back—get rid of you and *have David back*. And she wouldn't—she wouldn't—" He began to thump the wall in frustration.

Giles's face was expressionless. "Did she say why?"

"Why? Why? Who cares why? It was the perfect plan, and all she'd talk about was breaking hearts. As though breaking *your* heart would be a bad thing!"

"She was probably thinking of David," Giles observed with no sign of emotion.

"No—you, too. Said the kid loved you—you loved him—or something. Load of senti...sentimen...stupid rubbish. You really got your claws into her, didn't you?" His little eyes became cunning. "Once she'd have done anything I wanted. She was crazy about me. But now you—you..." He slammed his hand against the wall.

Giles watched the man in silence. Something was happening inside him, a turmoil of feeling that he was reluctant to examine too closely in case it proved an illusion. Everything this creature said pointed to one conclusion, but it was one he was afraid to take on trust. He'd trusted once before.

Oliver began to mumble again. "Thought she'd change her mind—went to see her again—nobody there. House shut up—neighbor said—Italy."

Giles kept very still lest the tumult inside him should be reflected on his face. "So the first time you talked to Melanie was before we went to Italy?" he asked casually.

"Ain't that what I just said? What difference anyway?"

It made all the difference, Giles thought, trying to stem the tide of rising excitement. It meant that Melanie had rejected the plan for recovering David before she could have been sure of marrying Giles. And that meant—his heart leapt as he thought what it might mean.

Oliver made a vague attempt at a conspiratorial wink and gave it up. "Shall I tell you just how stupid she was?" he offered.

"Yes, tell me," Giles said.

"I said—you can't deny I'm the father, not with that picture. Know what she said?" A sense of grievance almost sobered Oliver up, enabling him to speak coherently for a moment. "She said, 'But I can deny I'm his mother. See how much good your picture does you then?' I ask you! All that trouble to find him, and then she's going to deny it. Women!"

"There's no understanding them," Giles agreed in a soft voice. "But then, some of us aren't too clever in the way we go about it."

"What?"

"Nothing.

Giles regarded Oliver for a moment, as he might have looked at a slug. Then he went and called through the door for the sergeant.

"What you gonna do?" Oliver mumbled.

"I'm going to get you out of here," Giles said coldly. "And then I'm going to deal with you in my own way."

It was after midnight when he returned home, but Melanie was still up. "Is everything all right?" she asked, looking at his haggard face.

"I don't know. I've just been to the railway station to put a drunk aboard the night sleeper for Scotland, on a one-way ticket. He'll wake up three hundred miles away, wondering how he got there." He watched her face steadily. "His name's Oliver Dane." He saw her flinch and turn pale. "He's David's father, isn't he?"

"Yes. Giles, what has he been saying to you?"

"He's told me an interesting story about how he asked you to join forces with him to get David away from me."

"And you believed him?"

"I believe that he asked you."

"And you really think I'd have anything to do with such a plan?" she demanded passionately. "I sent him off with a flea in his ear. Giles, you've got to believe me."

He looked at her strangely. "Have I said that I don't?"

"No, but how do I know what's going on in your head? You think the worst of me so easily."

"Maybe. And maybe I'm a fool. Maybe I'm the biggest fool the world's ever seen. I just don't know."

Something in his voice, and even more in his eyes, made Melanie catch her breath. "What are you saying?" she whispered.

"Oliver Dane was drunk enough to tell the truth. He said you wouldn't help him."

"Did he tell you why?"

"Oh, yes. He despises your reasons as sentimental rubbish. He doesn't understand about not wanting to break people's hearts—David's or—mine." His eyes burned her. "Is it true, Melanie?"

"Yes, it's true. I saw what a strong bond there was between you and David. I couldn't hurt either of you by trying to break it. I love him, you know that. But I love you, too. Oh, why can't you believe me?"

"Perhaps I can. I want to. I want it so much—if you only knew how much!" His face was tortured. "Help me, Melanie. Help me believe."

She threw her arms about him, and for once she felt his answering embrace without constraint. His eager lips were on hers, telling her silently of his passion but also of his need for something more, the unconditional love he'd been denied all his life.

"I love you, Giles," she swore. "I'd never willingly do anything to hurt you. It wasn't just to get David, I swear it wasn't. Can't you believe me, after what Oliver told you?"

"I couldn't take in what I was hearing—that you had the chance to recover David, and turned it down. All the way home I've been trying to understand what it really meant. It's not just what Dane told me. I began to remember things about you. Since our marriage I've blinded myself to them, but the truth's been staring me in the face all the time. I should have known that instead of—"

"It doesn't matter," she said quickly.

"Oh, yes, it matters, because I need you to forgive me. Whatever happens to us now, I can't go on without forgiveness."

Whatever happens now. The words showed her that they were at a crossroads. Happiness was within reach, but there was a little way to go yet. "Tell me what things you remembered," she said, her heart beating with hope.

"When we were in Italy, the way you kept drawing away from me. Why? Your only security lay in marrying me. Why did you keep your distance, Melanie?"

"Because I was falling in love with you. Can you understand that? If we loved each other, then it was terrible that I was deceiving you. I was so confused. I promised myself I'd tell you at the right moment, but it never came. At least—it did once—"

"Tell me," he said, very pale.

"That weekend we spent alone together here. I came so close to telling you everything one night, but then you started talking about your mother, and Zena, and how you'd never felt loved for yourself. How could I tell you after that? You'd have thought it had happened again, that all I wanted was David. But that wasn't true. Oh, Giles, please believe it wasn't true. I loved you, *you,* yourself. And after that I couldn't bear to tell you what would hurt you. I promised myself I'd make you so happy that I could tell you one day and it wouldn't matter."

He looked into her face, torn between longing to believe and fearing to believe. "It's too good to be true," he said. "I'm afraid it'll be snatched from me again."

"It never will be," she promised. "Oh, my love, can't we be a real family at last, all three of us loving each other? That would be the best thing in the world."

"All three of us loving each other," he repeated longingly. "If only—"

A faint call came from upstairs. "You'd better go to him," Giles said.

"You come, too."

"No, it's you he wants."

"Only to ask if you're home yet, I'm sure. He needs both of us, Giles, loving him, and loving each other."

"You go up. I'll come in a minute."

David was sitting up in bed when she went in. "You should be asleep," she said. "It's past midnight."

"Is Daddy home?"

"Yes, he came in a few minutes ago. Shall I send him in?"

"No." His hand stayed her. "I want you to finish the story."

"All right. Just a little more."

"No, I want you to *finish* it," he insisted.

By what telepathy had he understood that the story was reaching its resolution tonight, she wondered? But he knew. It was there in his trustful eyes, and now she knew what she must say.

"When Seraphina had wandered a long time, a bird flew over her, calling, 'Go home. You're not needed here.' The bird explained that Peter was no longer unhappy. He'd been rescued by a kind wizard, who'd taken him to his own cave, and cared for him."

Melanie heard a step outside, then a faint creak as if the door were being pushed open. She didn't turn her head. She was totally aware of Giles, without needing to see him.

"Tell me about the wizard," David begged.

Before Melanie could speak, Giles said, "For many years he'd lived in a cold desert. He'd been there so long that he'd forgotten that there was anywhere else. Then he found Peter and his desert began to flower, but only a little, because Peter's heart was somewhere else. He longed for Seraphina, and every day he asked the wizard, 'Is she here yet? When will she come?'" Giles's eyes held David's as he spoke the words they would both remember, and he came into the room to stand behind Melanie.

"What happened?" David asked, watching them both intently.

"One day, she found them," Giles said. The slight pressure of his fingers on Melanie's shoulder told her that he wanted her to take up the tale.

"And when she saw Peter," she said, "he was exactly as she'd seen him in the pool. They knew each other at once, and ran to embrace. But when Seraphina said, 'Let us go home now,' Peter said, 'What about my wizard? He'll be sad without me.'

"At that moment the wizard came out of his cave. And when Seraphina saw him she began to understand that while she'd been searching for Peter, she'd also been searching for the wizard, without knowing it. Now she'd found him, and in that same instant, she loved him."

"What about the wizard?" David asked hopefully. "Did he love her?"

"Yes," Giles said. "Just as she'd been searching for him, he'd been waiting for her. When she came, his desert truly flowered." Giles's voice grew soft and urgent, making his words not only a declaration but a plea. "And he loved her with all his heart."

"And did they all stay together?" David persisted.

Melanie nodded, smiling. Her heart was so full that she could hardly speak, but she knew she must finish the story and make their miracle complete.

"Seraphina spoke to the wizard," she said. "She begged him, 'Let us all three live together in the Land of Heart's Joy.' Then they each took one of Peter's hands, and the three of them went away together, back to the Land of Heart's Joy, where they lived forever, and were never parted again.'"

She held her breath as Giles knelt down beside them. Suddenly David leapt up in bed, flung one arm about Melanie and the other about Giles. With an overflow-

ing heart Melanie embraced them both, feeling her
husband and son cling to her, united in their love and
need of her.

And so the three of them discovered the Land of
Heart's Joy, where they lived forever and were never
parted again.

* * * * *

COMING NEXT MONTH

**#985 THE BEAUTY, THE BEAST AND THE BABY—
Dixie Browning**

Tall, Dark and Handsome
March's *Man of the Month*, gorgeous Gus Wydowski, didn't
need anyone—especially a beautiful woman with a baby. But
Mariah Brady soon had him longing for a family to call his own....

#986 THE LAST GROOM ON EARTH—Kristin James
Angela Hewitt vowed she'd never fall for sexy Bryce Richards's
charm—even if he were the last man on earth. But when he came
to her rescue, falling for Bryce was the *least* of her troubles....

#987 RIDGE: THE AVENGER—Leanne Banks

Sons and Lovers
It was bad enough Ridge Jackson was hired to protect feisty
Dara Seabrook—now he was finding it impossible to resist her!
Ridge could have any woman he wanted; why then did he want
Dara, the one woman who might never be his?

#988 HUSBAND: OPTIONAL—Marie Ferrarella

The Baby of the Month Club
When Jackson Cain returned to town, he was shocked to discover
a very pregnant Mallory Flannigan. And though she claimed the
child wasn't his, Jackson was sure she was hiding something!

#989 ZOE AND THE BEST MAN—Carole Buck

Wedding Belles
Zoe Armitage wanted a husband and kids, not a rugged bachelor
who'd never settle down! Gabriel Flynn stole her heart, but would
he ever abandon his wandering ways to make Zoe his wife?

#990 JUST A MEMORY AWAY—Helen R. Myers
Free-spirited Frankie Jones was crazy about the mysterious man
she found suffering from amnesia. But once he discovered his
true identity, would he hightail it out of town for good?

Bestselling author

RACHEL LEE

takes her Conard County series to new heights with

A CONARD COUNTY *Reckoning*

This March, Rachel Lee brings readers a brand-new, longer-length, out-of-series title featuring the characters from her successful Conard County miniseries.

Janet Tate and Abel Pierce have both been betrayed and carry deep, bitter memories. Brought together by great passion, they must learn to trust again.

"Conard County is a wonderful place to visit! Rachel Lee has crafted warm, enchanting stories. These are wonderful books to curl up with and read. I highly recommend them."
—*New York Times* bestselling author
Heather Graham Pozzessere

Available in March, wherever Silhouette books are sold.

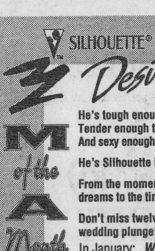

Yo amo novelas con corazón!

Starting this March, Harlequin opens up to a whole new world of readers with two new romance lines in SPANISH!

Harlequin Deseo
- passionate, sensual and exciting stories

Harlequin Bianca
- romances that are fun, fresh and very contemporary

With four titles a month, each line will offer the same wonderfully romantic stories that you've come to love—now available in Spanish.

Look for them at selected retail outlets.

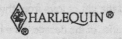

HARLEQUIN®

SPANT